BECOMING LOVERS

"You must know you're a beautiful and desirable woman."

"Then why haven't you gotten physical? You haven't even kissed me."

"I'm not sure I want to torture myself that way, Lanie. We're not kids you know. I want to make love to you, but not with a floor shift between us. I want the whole bit, in bed."

Now his hand progressed up to her arm and across, where his fingers performed a sensuous, stroking ritual. For the first time in over a year Lanie thought seriously of sex, actually longed for it.

"Do we go to your place or mine?"

"Yours," she said without preamble.

Other Avon Books by
Patricia Gallagher

THE THICKET

PATRICIA GALLAGHER

AVON
PUBLISHERS OF BARD, CAMELOT AND DISCUS BOOKS

THE THICKET is an original publication of Avon Books.

AVON BOOKS
A division of
The Hearst Corporation
959 Eighth Avenue
New York, New York 10019

First Avon Printing, November, 1973
Third Printing

AVON TRADEMARK REG. U.S. PAT. OFF. AND
FOREIGN COUNTRIES, REGISTERED TRADEMARK—
MARCA REGISTRADA, HECHO EN CHICAGO, U.S.A.

Printed in the U.S.A.

CONTENTS

THE THICKET

PART I: LANIE

"There are many kinds of thickets, and they grow in many places. Some grow wild in the country. Some are cultivated in humanity. Nature's thicket is easy to recognize. Man's is a little more difficult."

AN EVANGELIST'S HANDBOOK
TERRENCE SPENCER (1887-1939)

CHAPTER ONE

"Here, let me help you with that."

She turned abruptly, thinking she was alone. A sudden apparition couldn't have frightened her more than a strange voice. "You startled me!"

"I'm terribly sorry. You didn't see or hear me?" He smiled apologetically, but she was too frozen with fear to respond. "I came from the opposite direction. My car is parked at the rear entrance."

Her eyes scanned the back gate partially obscured by rank growth, glimpsed a late model yellow sports car, returned to his face. She had never seen him before. Woodlanders knew one another at least by sight, and a stranger was apt to attract attention on the street and create suspicion, speculation, and even alarm in the cemetery. It was an ideal spot for ambush, isolated at the edge of the forest, its wilderness eternally encroaching, so that annual grave cleanings had to be dedicated community projects, generally all-day family affairs like picnics, with food and drink and youngsters running and playing among the tombstones.

Lanie glanced furtively at her own car, estimating the distance and her chances of reaching it, locking the doors, and escaping. Hardly. He could easily overtake her. He was tall and his stride

11

would be long and swift. Besides, he was already
near enough to touch her if inclined. She decided
to stand firm and bluff—fake it, her teenager would
say. Actually, he did not appear desperate, degenerate, or dangerous, although she knew that appearances, as manners, could be and often were
deceiving.

"Kenneth Steele," he introduced himself.

"Lanine Hall," she reciprocated, cagily ignoring
the proffered handshake.

"Your late husband?"

A wary nod and peering eyes endeavoring to
penetrate whatever façade he was affecting, if any.
Not clairvoyance, however, merely simple deduc-
tion, since the vital statistics were legibly carved
in the marble monument. Brian Tyson Hall had
been dead over a year, and this would have been
his thirty-seventh birthday. His widow was paying
tribute with flowers and meditation, which the
stranger had interrupted.

"I'm looking for the graves of my great-grandparents," he stated. "Matthew and Sybil Steele.
Some family records indicate they might possibly
be here, in Woodland."

"I don't believe I've ever seen the names on any
of the markers, Mr. Steel." She was positive, in
fact.

"Perhaps they didn't have markers, or they were
removed or destroyed somehow. It was long ago."

"Longer ago than 1857?" asked Lanie, still apprehensive. "That's when this town was founded."

"I realize a lot can happen in that length of time,
Mrs. Hall. But I have to start somewhere, and this
seemed the logical place."

Whatever his motives, Lanie was sufficiently intrigued to indulge him—rare in itself, for she was

12

not the kind of woman easily charmed or persuaded by a fascinating man. Certainly she had known equally attractive men, and some even more so. He was almost too dark, hair and eyes black, skin deeply-tanned. But Brian had been swarthy too from outdoor activity, with similar strong features, and perhaps it was this vague resemblance that favorably impressed her. Gradually her fears subsided, ultimately vanished. After all, he'd had ample opportunity to attack. It was really paranoid to be so suspicious of strangers—a trait undoubtedly inherited from her conservative mother, whose caution in this respect made Lanie seem reckless. But this one appeared legitimate enough, relatively harmless, and even worth cultivating.

"May I do that for you, ma'am?"

"Please." Lanie surrendered the pitcher she'd brought along to fill the Grecian urns flanking the massive memorial, which suddenly seemed formidable and pretentious even for an industrial giant and favorite community son. "There's a hydrant over there, by that spiral cedar."

"I see it."

His receding figure cast a substantial shadow, proving he was not the specter she had first imagined. Drawing water, he returned and filled the vessels, while Lanie divided and arranged the immense bouquet of roses, lilies, and fern.

"Beautiful," he remarked. "From your garden?"

"My mother's. Unfortunately, they won't last long in this heat. They're wilting already."

"It's the thought that counts."

"So they say, but sometimes I think the living comfort themselves primarily with these gestures. Rituals, rather, performed out of habit as much as tribute."

Such a thought would not have occurred to her yesterday, nor even an hour ago, and it disturbed her now. She hesitated before saying the brief silent prayer that always concluded her visits. His presence, bare head respectfully bowed, was somehow incongruous and ironical, if not profane. There was no reason to linger further, and no attempt on his part to detain her, yet she couldn't leave. She moved as if magnetically drawn into the shade of a moss-shrouded liveoak. Nearby a pyramidal magnolia stood green-robed and majestic. But the princely pine was the true monarch of the land, patriarchal, providing its livelihood and sustenance.

He followed, uninvited. "In New Orleans we bury above ground generally. Drainage problems. It's below sea level."

"I know. I've been there many times. The cemeteries are tourist attractions."

"Only the French Quarter draws more visitors, and Mark Twain once said that New Orleans' best architecture was to be found in its graveyards."

"I take it New Orleans is your home?"

"At present. I'm not sure for how long, though. It's rather lonely since I lost my wife."

Lanie tensed again, wondering if he expected sympathy, or to establish rapport through commiseration. She only said, "I'm sorry."

"That's life—and life is for the living, isn't it?" A realistic shrug, a pause to consider the beauty and vitality of living nature around them. "This part of Texas is similar to western Louisiana—not surprising, since only a river separates us. That makes us neighbors, Mrs. Hall."

"About your family, Mr. Steele—have you checked our county records?"

"I tried, but the vital statistics don't go back that

14

far. I understand the courthouse burned in 1918, destroying all previous documents."

Lanie had forgotten that fire, it being considerably before her time.

"That's true. Federal census records and tombstones supplied prior data. Residents furnished more, which means its accuracy depends largely on memory and notations in family Bibles and journals. Some folks probably fudged a bit on their ages and grew younger. Others may have seized the opportunity to disappear entirely."

"And there being no living Steeles here at the time to account for themselves, they were naturally omitted." He frowned at his plight. "All I have to go on is the entry in an old diary, which lists Woodland County or its environs as their last known residence. I'm just assuming they lived, died, and were buried in this general vicinity."

Lanie wanted to help him, curious as to why it should be important to him at this late date. Did he need proof to contest a will and establish his inheritance by succession? Was he a private detective conducting a missing heirs investigation? A writer compiling a regional history? Or simply, as he had stated, interested in locating his ancestors? Genealogy was, after all, the third most popular hobby in the world, next to coin and stamp collecting. And some local citizens, notably Mrs. Arthur Whitney, were absorbed in it.

"My mother is active in our historical society," Lanie volunteered, "and their records are intact. They combine fact and lore, however, and it's often difficult to distinguish between them. But if anyone could help you, Mother could. Would you like to meet her, Mr. Steele?"

"I'd be delighted, Mrs. Hall."

"Are you free for dinner this evening?"

"Oh, don't go to any trouble."

Lanie fanned herself with a scented handkerchief. Even under the dense green umbrella, the semitropical sun was intense, depleting, and there wasn't enough breeze to flutter the long parasitic veils of mauve-gray moss, which hung like irridescent illusion veils.

"No trouble if you don't mind potluck."

"You live with your mother?"

"And my daughter. Beth recently celebrated a milestone birthday—she's sweet sixteen." Now why had she added that information? A woman her age could easily have a teenage child. Anyway, it was none of his business.

"What time, Mrs. Hall?"

"Time?"

"Dinner, ma'am."

"Oh. Eightish."

"And the address?"

Lanie flushed in embarrassment; she was behaving like a flustered schoolgirl, forgetting details. "Nine thirty-nine Pine Road. Whitney House. You can't miss it. But if you should, anyone in town can direct you. May I ask where you're staying, in case I should have to cancel or something?"

"The Fiesta Motel."

"But that's miles out on the highway!"

"I didn't know what I'd find closer in."

"Nothing much better, I'm afraid. This isn't exactly a metropolis, merely an overgrown sawmill town." Extending her hand, and smiling encouragingly she said, "Nice meeting you, Mr. Steele. We'll expect you this evening."

She strolled self-consciously to her Lincoln Continental, wishing ardently that she were wearing something other than tailored slacks and an old blouse. The weather had probably wrecked her hair and makeup, too; she felt wilted, melted, smeared. One last glance assured her that he hadn't vanished as unexpectedly as he'd appeared. Sun glinting off marble and granite blurred her eyes, nearly blinding her, but happily he was still visible, smiling benignly under the shadow of the oak. She waved a gloveless hand. Surely Brian wouldn't mind, if such things could possibly matter to him now. Surely it had been long enough, and too long.

In any small community the doctor's house is well known. If several generations of physicians have occupied the same address, it is famous. Such was Whitney House, a classic Southern Colonial whose white clapboard walls had sheltered three generations of M.D.s, and was still referred to as "the doctor's house," although none was in residence now, the tradition having ended with the death of Lanie's father, Dr. Arthur Whitney.

Mrs. Whitney was at the heirloom mahogany secretary in the largely medical library, tallying some household accounts. At sixty-three, Eunice was still attractive, healthy, active, and financially secure. She kept busy with church, clubs, garden, community projects, plus her particular pets— history and conservation. By comparison, her daughter was languid and leisurely, lacking both the older woman's energy and enthusiasm for life.

Eunice accepted her widowhood with grace, resignation, and serenity. When Lanie lost her husband she underwent a severe emotional crisis that required psychotherapy in Houston. Mrs. Whitney visited her husband's grave on special anniversaries. The frequency of her daughter's pilgrimages had already become a legend in town. Anyone determined to meet the younger widow would have known precisely where to find her and when.

"I was getting worried about you, dear. You've been gone longer than usual. Anything wrong?"

"No, I just met a man."

"Man? What man, and where?"

Lanie explained, including the spontaneous invitation, which elevated her mother's brows suspiciously.

"You've been in the sun too long, perhaps. Sit down, darling. Are you having headaches again?"

During the first six months of her bereavement Lanie had experienced frequent excruciating migraines, diagnosed as psychosomatic. They had decreased as she adjusted to her loss and ultimately disappeared. She resented the reference to them now, as if she were unstable again.

"It's not sunstroke, Mother, I'm not hallucinating, and I haven't had a migraine in months."

"No offense, dear. But you must admit picking up a stray in a cemetery and inviting him home for a meal isn't exactly the most rational or discreet behavior. This isn't a goodwill mission, you know."

"And he's not a derelict, Mother. I told you why he was there. I thought possibly you could help him."

"And I've told you, those names are not in the least familiar to me. If they'd ever lived here and were anybody at all, I'd have heard of them, don't you think? So would you and a lot of other people."

"So maybe they were nobodies? Is that a sin or crime?"

"Lanine darling, people do not spend their entire lives in a community of this size without being known to someone, unless they were invisible—and I assume they were not ghosts or phantoms. This person is obviously mistaken, either about the place or the time. Or he has some scheme in mind."

Anticipating that reaction, Lanie was prepared for it. "He didn't say they had spent their entire lives here, Mother, only that it was their last known address. And he's already inquired at the courthouse. But of course the registers prior to August, 1918, burned in the fire—an historical fact of which *he* had to remind *me*."

"Logical if he's telling the truth," Eunice surmised. "Convenient if he isn't. Clever in any event."

"Oh, good grief, Mother! Why should a stranger come to a place like this to lie about dead relatives?"

"You might ask yourself that question."

"I have, and it doesn't make sense."

"Not to you, perhaps. But it may to Kenneth Steele, if that's his real name. Could be an alias, and could be he's more interested in your heritage than his."

Lanie sighed, grimacing. "You'd suspect Howard Hughes of ulterior motives."

"And the Pope, if he approached you under those circumstances. Peculiar, to say the least."

"Why, for God's sake? You've traced Dad's ancestors to a Magna Carta scribe, and yours to Genesis. And at least two recent Presidents have journeyed overseas to try to locate the graves of forefathers. What's so peculiar about an ordinary citizen traveling a few hundred miles in search of his?"

"He might be president someday and need the information for his memoirs?" Mrs. Whitney smiled at her child's naïveté. "There's nothing wrong with anyone's interest in his ancestry, Lanie. It's admirable, and I'd be the last to deny it. I've spent innumerable hours in such research myself, of course. And a cemetery is an ideal place to launch a genealogical voyage into the past. But it can take months, years, to establish authentic identity and lineage. No vine of nature can become more entangled than the family tree. Granted that Mr. Steel might be honestly motivated, I'd like some tangible proof of his sincerity. If he brought along that family record or whatever and will permit me to examine it at length, I'll be convinced, or at least less skeptical. Was he surprised to be invited here rather than to your home?"

"Why should he be? I doubt if he knows it exists."

"One needn't live in London to have heard of Buckingham Palace, my dear."

"The Hall Estate is hardly in that class, Mother."

"It is in this area, and you can bet your coffers he's aware of it."

"And to think the Halls were nobodies when they came here a century ago," Lanie said cynically. "I wonder if the Historical Society would have bothered with their biographies if they hadn't been so successful? Bought timberland for pennies and started a sawmill that developed into one of the world's largest lumber operations. If the shrewd old patriarch of the clan hadn't migrated from Maine to Texas in an ox cart to begin with, built a log cabin and fought off Indians and sired adventurous offspring who gambled on anything that promised a profit? If they hadn't become 'worthwhile' people by your standards?"

"All right, Lanie, I'm chastised. And perhaps I should be grateful to this stranger, whoever he is—

grateful to anyone who could resurrect your spirit if even only temporarily from mourning. I was beginning to fear you'd entombed yourself with Brian for eternity. You've given every eligible bachelor in the state frostbite."

"They weren't all eligible bachelors, Mother."

"And this one is different?"

"He's a widower," Lanie replied quietly. "We have something in common, anyway."

"Indeed? That's interesting. What happened to the late Mrs. Steele?"

"Presumably she died. How else could he become a widower?"

"On, there are other ways, some quite ingenious."

Lanie laughed. "You've been reading too many mysteries, Mother. Now I think I'd better go warn Maple. She may need to whip up extra dessert or something ..."

CHAPTER TWO

Not since the tragedy that had devastated her at
thirty-four had Lanie spoken and moved with such
vitality and alacrity. And she had actually dressed
for dinner, discarding her almost habitual slacks
for a soft blue silk dress. If nothing else the man
had revived her pride and femininity, her sexual
awareness, and for this minor miracle Mrs. Whitney
was grateful.

She had despaired of her daughter's emergence
from her voluntary shell, although the psychiatrist
had assured her it was a natural seclusion and
rarely permanent; sorrowing souls were apt to retreat in solitude. Now she had emerged—and of all
unlikely coaxers, a transient in a cemetery! Eunice
would have thought it fantasy or delusion, except
that Lanie had not suffered these symptoms even
in the extremes of depression, despair, and anxiety.
And she had been released from therapy several
months ago, bearing out Dr. Harmon's prognosis
of temporary neurosis.

"Congratulations, dear. You're a woman again
and lovely as ever. I'd almost forgotten how lovely."

"Thanks," Lanie murmured. But she was nervous
as a child awaiting the arrival of a package sent

home on approval, afraid the merchandise might not meet with parental approval. She had not made an important decision in so long, she had lost confidence in her own judgment.

"Is Elizabeth joining us for dinner?"

"Yes, and please don't call her Elizabeth tonight, Mother. You know how she hates it. Just call her Beth. She's getting ready now."

"Pants, naturally?"

"Naturally."

Mrs. Whitney sighed. "I wish someone could charm *her* out of them. Oh, dear! That didn't come out right, did it?"

"Not quite," Lanie said as the door chimes pealed. "He's here, Mother."

"Punctual, anyway. Well, let him in, Lanine. I'm anxious to meet this Louisiana marvel."

Kenneth Steele exceeded her expectations. Lanie had said he resembled Brian slightly, but Eunice didn't agree. Descended from rural stock, as most East Texans, Brian Hall had retained some rough edges beneath an acquired patina of sophistication, and much of his imposing stature had been sheer physical bulk.

Steele was tall and well built, but not bulky. Physically there was as much difference between them as between the bear and panther all the Doctors Whitney had hunted in the Big Thicket.

"Welcome to Woodland and Whitney House, Mr. Steele."

"Thank you for receiving me, Mrs. Whitney."

Impeccable manners which could be rehearsed. No distinguishable accent or dialect, and his facial features might be French, Acadian, Spanish, Creole, almost anything. Somewhat too dark for her taste—

but some of the fairest women admired brunette men, considered them masculine.

"My daughter has told me about your quest, Mr. Steele, and I'm afraid I can't help you. I'm familiar with the history of this region, having helped compile much of it, and I'm sorry to say I've no knowledge of any Matthew or Sybil Steele. Do you have that family diary or whatever with you?"

"Unfortunately not. It's very old and fragile, partially written in French, with entries predating the Civil War, and my aunt won't let it out of her sight. She thinks it's a valuable manuscript if nothing else."

"I should think so, too," Mrs. Whitney said. "Any document of that vintage is valuable. Have the French passages been translated?"

"Those that were legible, yes. My aunt is a retired school teacher. French was one of her subjects. I also read and speak it, although not fluently. Some pages are missing, however, and others have insertions and deletions, which make deciphering difficult. More than one person wrote in the record, you see."

"My, it does sound like a challenge," Eunice said. "But you're determined?"

"Why yes, I am." He seemed puzzled, as if he'd missed part of the conversation and was waiting for a cue.

"Yet you've never been here before?"

"I only recently discovered the journal," he explained, "in an old trunk in Aunt Selma's attic. She's my father's sister and had forgotten the diary herself for many years. I was looking for some lost legal papers when I found it."

Embarrassed by the maternal third degree, Lanie tried to divert or diminish it. "Mother has a crowded attic, too. I imagine there're some surprises stored up there; I must rummage some day."

Beth bounced downstairs then, buoyant as a bright rubber ball. Bell-bottoms, yellow fringed tunic, multicolor Indian beads. Dark smooth hair touching her waist, luminous gray eyes in a sepia-tanned face. Elizabeth Hall was her father's child, as vibrantly dark as her mother was radiantly fair. The buckskin moccasins were in deference to company; she preferred bare feet.

"My daughter Beth," Lanie introduced her. "This is Mr. Kenneth Steele, darling."

"How are you, Beth?"

She gave him a cursory appraisal, unimpressed with his straight apparel. And for once she was inclined to agree with her grandmother: a graveyard was an unlikely place to meet. Hordes of tourists passed through Woodland, however, en route to the Big Thicket and the Indian Reservation, which Beth was currently promoting. If this were his destination, she might try to establish contact and rapport, otherwise it didn't seem worth the effort.

"Making it, I guess," she replied. "You?"

"Trying," he said.

The remark drew a grin from the girl. "I hear you're on a relative scavenger hunt. Why bother? Don't we all go back to Neanderthal? If you'd like to meet some genuine American aborigines—"

"Elizabeth," Eunice interrupted, "Mr. Steele is not here to espouse your cause, whatever it is this week."

"The same as last week, Grandma, and last year and the year before. Gee, what's keeping Maple? There's a Bogie flick on TV this evening, and I don't want to miss it. Maybe I better give the slave a hand in the galley—"

The meal was hardly potluck, but Steel hadn't expected it to be. Leftovers were not served in the formal dining rooms of elegant homes. And this one reminded him, although it was on a smaller scale, of his late wife's town house in the Garden District of New Orleans. Even the twilight scene beyond the glass French doors—magnificent old trees draped with mantillas of Spanish moss—was similar to the view from those Louisiana windows. Ironic how much even the landscapes had in common.

His hostess asked, "How long do you plan to stay in our town, Mr. Steele?"

"That depends, ma'am. I only arrived last night. Meeting Mrs. Hall was the sheerest luck, and when she said you might be able to help me—well, it was a long shot, but I had to take it."

"Oh, but I hope you won't give up," Lanie encouraged. "The search, I mean. Are you quite sure you have the right place, though. There's a Woodglade, Woodside, Woodedge, Woodbine, and others in this vicinity. It drives the Post Office mad."

"I can imagine," he said. "And I'm fairly certain that Woodland is the name listed in the journal, although the ink is faded and it's at the bottom of a leaf, like a footnote, and not mentioned again that I could see. If I don't succeed here, however, I'll investigate those other places."

"Godzilla!" cried Beth, spooning up her chocolate mousse and talking with her mouth full. "You're going to spend all that time and energy on such a project? It's not only flaky but unreal. Grandma's hung up on that moss, but you look more advanced."

"Speak English," Eunice admonished. "And don't spill your dessert on the tablecloth. Chocolate's hard to remove from linen without using those polluting detergents you want banned in this house."

Beth frowned, sobering. "I just don't see why anyone should really care about such things. I mean, what can you do about it, even if your sire was the Loch Ness Monster or King Kong or the Devil himself? You can't change your family tree—graft branches to suit yourself."

"Nevertheless, some people still do care, Elizabeth. And so should you, if your generation's as concerned with its identity as it pretends."

"Not *that* way, Grandma. Ancestry has nothing to do with it. It's who am I now, today, and where am I going now, today, tomorrow? An entirely different odyssey—get it?"

"I'm afraid not, child. The generation gap is a canyon here, and all I hear are empty echoes," she said and stood up. "We'll have coffee in the living room."

"I'll help Maple clear the table," Beth volunteered to escape that ritual. And giving the guest a peace sign and wink, "Don't take any wooden ancestors, man."

Ken smiled and almost winked back. He liked the girl, and thought her flippancy camouflaged a solid core character. Obviously she had a mind of her own and did not see herself in anyone else's image. He admired her mettle and individuality; but he'd also hate to cross purposes with her, or incur her opposition on any vital issue.

Maple brought the coffee on a silver tray. She was a light-skinned Negress who had served the family for thirty years, and Mrs. Whitney spoke of her proprietorially as "our Maple," even though she had a husband, a son in college, and a home of her own.

"Do you know anything about teenagers, Mr. Steele?"

"Not from personal experience, ma'am, since I have no children. But those of my friends pretty well conform to your granddaughter's pattern, with variations."

"She's in her Indian phase now," Lanie said, "which hopefully explains her wild clothes. Some people favor returning Texas to the Mexicans, but my daughter would give it back to the Indians. And she'll try to enlist your aid, if you let her." Sipping her coffee, she added "You still have Indians in your state, don't you?"

"More than in yours, I believe. A good many Houmas, some Choctaws and Chitimachas. And Coushattas."

Mrs. Whitney said, "Some of your Coushattas marry into our Alabama-Coushatta tribes, but they're not increasing very rapidly. I think it's their small numbers and the possibility of their extinction that fascinates our local youth most. The underdog, you know, has always been a popular cause with the young."

Lanie interrupted. "Mr. Steele has a more personal interest, Mother. Can't you lend him any assistance at all?"

"The Historical Society histories and biographies," Eunice offered magnanimously, "if he wants to read them."

Ken hesitated, "There doesn't seem to be much point, if they contain no reference to my relatives."

"Perhaps Mother missed something."

"Not likely, if she helped write them."

Mrs. Whitney touched her gray hair. "I'm not infallible, Mr. Steele, and you're welcome to study the records."

Ken thanked her by inviting the three of them to dine with him the next evening. Lanie accepted almost too quickly. Eunice excused herself via other plans, and Lanie would invent some for Beth, if necessary.

Abruptly he stood, obviously surprising his hostess who had expected him to overstay his welcome. "Now I think I've imposed enough on your hospitality, ma'am. If I might have those chronicles, I can start reading tonight."

"Yes, of course," Eunice said. "I'll get them for you. And take your time, sir—there's no hurry."

Immediately after he had gone, Lanie asked anxiously, "What do you think of him?"

"Does it matter?"

"Oh, Mother—he's nice, don't you think?"

"He seems to be a gentleman," Eunice allowed. "I wonder who his wife was?"

"I can't see how that's important now, Mother. She's dead. And if he wants to tell me about her, I'll listen. But I refuse to pry."

"That was a hand-tailored suit he was wearing," Eunice remarked. "Italian silk, I believe. Gold cuff links and an expensive wristwatch. Such things require money, Lanie. What kind of car does he drive?"

"Some little sport model, inexpensive."

"As compared to what—a Rolls?"

Lanie ignored that. "Why do you suppose he left so quickly? I hope we didn't bore or offend him somehow. You and your presumptuous questions, Mother! Asking how long he intended to stay in 'our' town, as if we owned it, and he was trespassing. That was incredibly rude, and I was mortified."

"Poor little butterfly. He's charmed you out of your cocoon, hasn't he? If that's charisma, he's loaded with it. But I'm not as susceptible as you. He didn't really want to take the records, you know. He reconsidered only because it would seem odd if he didn't."

"Oh, rot! You just made it seem useless, a waste of time to study them. And you still think he's playing some kind of game, don't you?"

"Not being clairvoyant, I can't say. But charade or not, obviously you want to play along with him. Just don't let him make all the rules, Lanine, insist on a few of your own. And watch out for tricks."

"Suspicion, thy name is Eunice," Lanie mocked. "Do you think Beth liked him?"

"Who can tell about that child? Lord, what a spectacle in that crazy costume! I'm not convinced that her interest in the Thicket tribes is just a phase, Lanine. I think she's been aware of them since I took her to the reservation when she was seven, because I thought it would be educational. Then she started collecting pictures and arrowheads and reading books about them. And the way she rides that horse and runs off by herself! Don't you see any smoke signals?"

"No, she's done that ever since Brian gave her that Apaloosa at ten. She's got a thing for horses."

Eunice frowned. "But she's growing up, Lanie. She's changed a great deal this past year, though you don't seem to realize it. Of course we've both had other problems to occupy us. Your illness and—"

"I'm all right now, Mother."

"Then, you'd better pay more attention to your daughter," Eunice advised. "She acts like a social renegade—those outlandish clothes and that unintelligible jargon she speaks half the time, not to mention her rebellious philosophies. And her mother not much better, taking up with a stranger in a cemetery, of all places! I should lock you both up."

"Why not just go to bed?" Lanie suggested. "I'm not at all sleepy. I'm going for a walk."

"Alone, at this hour? I'll go with you."

"Mother, please. I don't need a chaperone."

"Well, be careful and don't go far. There may be some tramps in the woods. Or transients," she added pointedly.

The winding street was lighted by an occasional arc lamp and the rising moon. Pine scented the night air like incense, but during the day it reeked of sawdust, resin, pulp, and hummed with the whines of ripsaws and the roars of trucks.

So vast and diversified were the Hall Industries that Lanie had only a small conception of what she and her daughter had actually inherited. Fortunately the estate, still in probate, was in the hands of competent attorneys and managers. Eventually, however, the heirs alone would have to make some disposition of the residence, which they had not occupied since the funeral.

Beth, who had seemed to love the place when small, now claimed to hate it as a representation of all the wrong values in life: wealth, power, influence, pretension. She suggested converting it to a charitable institution—orphanage, hospital, home for unwed mothers, ashram for intellectual pilgrims complete with live-in gurus, anything but the private monument she considered it. And where once she had enjoyed watching the lumber operations, she now deplored the felling of the trees, often weeping copiously, even though reforestation was a constant process, and many of the former regional farms, ranches, and cotton plantations now raised pines.

Lanie remembered one particularly sentimental occasion, when Beth had accused the Halls of being a dynasty of destroyers. "That's our family occupation, Mother. Destruction, and it's our heritage. Those lumber trucks are nature's hearses and their sounds her funeral dirge."

"There'd be no buildings and newsprint without them, darling. Some things must perish for others to exist—it's an old law of nature. Would you prefer to live in caves and read stone tablets? Even the Indians destroyed trees for shelter and firewood, and animals for food and hides."

"They did it to survive; we do it for money. Greed and profit and to perpetuate the System."

"Oh, Bethie baby, you sound like a rubber stamp for the Now Generation! Try to be a little more original."

"You're as bad as Grandma, except that she can't seem to understand, and you don't seem to want to, Mother."

Now another issue had risen between them, and Lanie hoped it would not become a wedge to wrench them apart completely. Beth's initial reaction to Kenneth Steele had been vague and inconclusive. Neither positive nor negative, as far as she could determine, merely neutral.

Lanie had reached the end of Pine Road and was ready to turn back, when she saw his car still in the neighborhood. Apparently he had lost his way, which was easy to do, with the lanes meandering through the forest like cattle and Indian trails, as some were, ending in circles and cul de sacs. Difficult enough for natives to orient, much less a stranger in the dark. Amusing, actually. A traveler embarked on a journey into the past should have a better sense of direction, and she just might tease him about it tomorrow. . . .

CHAPTER THREE

"Have any trouble finding your way last night?" Lanie asked as they were seated in a candlelit booth at the Stage-coach Inn, advertised as Woodland's finest restaurant.

"A little," he admitted sheepishly. "Took a wrong turn somewhere and ended up going in circles. How did you know?"

"Oh, I'm not psychic! Even the natives occasionally get confused and lost. You're in the tall Texas timbers, Stranger. Just don't wander westward into the Big Thicket. Some people never come out."

"So I've heard. The proprietor of the Fiesta Motel seems to be an authority on the Thicket. He briefed me over breakfast and lunch. I understand there's a campaign on now to make it into a National Park—a bill has already been introduced in the Senate."

"The vanishing wilderness pitch," Lanie nodded, "and I'm weary of it. A Supreme Court justice helped to get it started, and naturally the politicians jumped on the band wagon. Ecology is a popular cause now, and park status would be a boom to the tourist business. But the Thicket's a long way from extinction, and the lumber industry can't be blamed for all the so-called desecrations and decimations."

"That sounds defensive?"

"It is, and unfortunately I have to defend the Halls against the accusations from one of their own. My daughter constantly indicts her father. Isn't that fanatic?"

"Not necessarily."

"*Et tu, Brute?*" she mocked.

Ken consulted the menu. The specialty was prime ribs of beef, which on Lanie's recommendation he ordered along with vintage burgundy. "I did some reading last night," he said, "but didn't turn up anything useful to me. If the Steeles ever lived here, they didn't leave discernible tracks. Either they were lightfooted, or very mediocre."

"Which makes them like the majority of people, doesn't it?"

"Also difficult to trace. Unlike the Halls with their giant steps, or the Whitneys with their professional ones."

"Are you on vacation, Ken?" They had progressed to informality."

"Partially."

"May I ask what you do for a living?"

"I'm an investment counselor. I was formerly with my father-in-law's brokerage firm in New Orleans. That's how I met my late wife. Michele was Peter Danielle's daughter and only child. After her death, I left the company and opened my own office. It's small, but growing, thanks to some of the old gentleman's clients who defected to me."

"Primarily female?"

His eyes confronted hers a little angrily. "Sex has nothing to do with stocks and bonds, my dear. They're neuter gender. But since women outlive men, they consequently are the principal investors. It's a natural phenomenon for which I'm not responsible. However, I'm pleased to say that some wealthy ladies do value my judgment and entrust their portfolios to me. Enough so that I had to take in a partner to allow myself some leisure. He's minding the store now."

"That's nice," Lanie said. "Fortunately managers handle the Hall investments. I know absolutely nothing about such matters. My husband was the financial brain of the family."

She had not intended to mention Brian at all this evening, to dredge up any painful memories whatever, yet it seemed a normal sequence in the process of acquaintance. And she hoped for reciprocation, since she was more curious about the late Mrs. Steele than she cared to admit even to herself.

"Spared you all the dull details, did he?"

"As many as possible, anyway. That's what a husband should do, don't you think?"

"Not according to Women's Lib," he said, then added, "It must have been quite a jolt when he was suddenly gone?"

"Devastating," Lanie admitted. "And of course I was helpless as the proverbial clinging vine suddenly deprived of its solid support. He was returning from a business trip to Baton Rouge when his plane crashed."

"Yes, I remember. Louisiana authorities weren't sure he'd cleared our woods before he went down. The search was news until the wreckage was found. Naturally there was an investigation? Was the cause definitely established? Mechanical failure, pilot error, what?"

"Possibly both, in addition to the turbulence that carried him off course. Brian drove himself mercilessly, never taking enough time to rest. He should have spent that stormy night in Baton Rouge, but I guess he was anxious to get home. It was a nightmare for me—the waiting, uncertainty, and hideous climax." The appalling vigil was still vivid in her mind: six long days of searching in the dense East Texas forests before the plane was discovered half-submerged in a cypress swamp. She had simply collapsed at the news.

"Ironically, my wife's death was also accidental," he volunteered. "She was water skiing on Lake Ponchartrain. The towline broke and apparently one of the skis struck her head. I was steering the boat and couldn't get to her fast enough. I've had my share of nightmares too, believe me. The self-recrimination variety. If I'd maneuvered swifter, if I'd reached her sooner, if, if, if. Sometimes I think that word was invented primarily to torture people."

"Were you alone in the boat?"

He nodded gravely. "We had a house on the lake and frequently spent our weekends there. With friends sometimes, but that day we were alone. There wasn't even another boat near enough on the water to lend assistance. Somehow I managed to get Michele into ours and administered artificial respiration and mouth-to-mouth resuscitation. But it was too late, she was gone. When I finally got her to a hospital, it was hopeless. The pathologist who did the autopsy said she had drowned, probably rendered unconscious by the ski blow first."

"How awful," Lanie murmured.

He stared at the rare meat the waiter had just placed before him. "I'm sorry if I've depressed you."

Over the flickering candleflame, Lanie said, "I'm

afraid it was inevitable, Ken, the reference to our late mates. I think we just had to mention them."

"I suppose," he brooded.

"Do you still have your lake property?"

"Yes, but it's for sale. I can't bear it now. And our town house belonged to her family, so naturally I vacated it as soon as possible. I live in an apartment in one of those huge impersonal complexes. But it's not bad. Modern conveniences and no sad memories."

Lanie understood and sympathized, for it was essentially the reason she had left the palatial home Brian had built for her, that great white elephant in its landscaped jungle. "Do you believe in fate, Ken?"

"I did once. And Michele, always. She was interested in occultism, too. There's a lot of it in New Orleans, you know, and more in the Bayou Country. Mysticism was sort of a hobby with Michele—she had many hobbies. I know she believed in reincarnation and thought she possessed strong ESP. If so, it wasn't strong to warn her about that weak rope." He tasted the wine, approved, and proceeded to carve the bloody beef, which might have come from a Hall-branded steer, since ranches were included in the farflung empire.

Lanie was still on her salad, wondering what evil connotations her mother would attach to the information he'd just imparted, wondering if she even dared to relay it.

"How far did you get in the *History of Woodland County*?" she asked.

"Far enough to know we're sitting on the original site of the Butterfield, Wells Fargo, and Pony Express station," he replied. "Did you win the bet with your mother?"

Candleglow camouflaged Lanie's blush. "I wasn't testing you, Ken. Anyway, you could have gotten that information from the yellow pages of the local telephone directory. The Chamber of Commerce is very proud of the 'authentic atmosphere' of this place. Some of the lamps actually are from stagecoaches, and those are genuine passenger tickets, bills of lading, and saddle mailbags on display in the lobby."

"Really? Maybe I wasted the midnight oil reading the wrong directory." He smiled perceptively. "Beware of strangers, daughter. The maternal edict since time immemorial, and natural enough. Mary's mother probably cautioned her against Joseph. 'A carpenter from Nazareth? Mercy, Mary! What's he after?' "

"Was Mother all that transparent? She's usually more subtle."

"It doesn't matter," he said. "I don't expect to be around long enough to discomfit her. More wine? Dessert? There's a pastry list."

"Just wine, please." She needed the fortification, not the stimulation. His personality was intoxicating enough, demanding emotional response; she felt a rapport with him that aroused sensations dormant since the tragedy that had transformed her from wife to widow.

Replenishing her glass, he observed, "You're not eating, Lanie. Don't you like the food? I'm no gourmet, but I consider it excellent. I don't believe Antoine's could prepare better prime ribs."

"I'm glad you're enjoying it. We have a good seafood restaurant also, and that's about it. You can see why the merchants are trying to promote tourism. Not all residents support them, however.

You can bring in too many undesirable elements that way."

"Opportunists?"

"And worse. Riffraff. Rabble."

"The community is free of it now?"

"Comparatively. There haven't been any such parasites since Spindletop blew in, and all East Texas became a prospector's paradise. Bogus oil leases and stocks were peddled the way gold and silver securities were in other times. The senior citizens say Woodland was a boom town then, as wild and lawless as in its rawest frontier days. But that's long since over, and it's calm and conservative now."

"And the natives know their respective places, right? The minorities don't mingle and spread the blight. How complacent the Old Guard must feel to be in secure command again."

"Oh, heavens! I didn't mean to discriminate, Ken. The people are just inhibited and close-knit. The clan system still survives here. In fact, it's a way of life."

"Clan, or caste?"

"Dear me, how did we get off on this sticky tangent?" She laughed a little nervously and abruptly changed the subject. "What do you think of my daughter?"

"Live wire."

"You mean shocking?"

"No, just alive."

"Well, I must admit she shocks me sometimes. And her grandmother most of the time."

"I can imagine."

"Mother is inclined to forget that every generation has its follies. Hers was the Charleston and bootleg liquor, although she swears she never indulged in either. But moonshine stills flourished in the Big Thicket during Prohibition, and I don't doubt Woodlanders consumed their share, even the professed teetotalers. Now, it's rock festivals and pot and God-knows-what, but I'm satisfied that Beth isn't involved in any such craziness. Her dedication seems to be Indians and ecology."

"Could be worse," Ken said.

"I reckon. But she's too young for such serious interests. A girl her age should concentrate on more frivolous things—pretty clothes, friends, fun. Beth is too old for her years, and too intense. I should have sent her away to school, but was afraid of exposing her prematurely to the new youth culture. Unfortunately, it's everywhere, like the prevailing winds. Beth lost the stabilizing influence of a father just when she needed him most. Be glad you weren't left with an adolescent child to raise alone, Ken. Believe me, it's difficult."

"I'm sure it is, Lanie."

After dinner they drove around for awhile, circling the square a few times, Lanie showing him what little Woodland had to offer and half-expecting to arrive at the motel on some pretext or other, if not actual proposition. To her surprise he brought her home before midnight and did not even attempt to kiss her goodnight or arrange another date. Had she misjudged his initial interest? She hadn't been so worried about her sex appeal since her hair was in a ponytail and her teeth in braces.

Not surprisingly, however, Eunice had waited up for her, pretending to be engrossed in a new novel. "Home so early? I didn't expect you for hours. My, he is clever."

Lanie was in no mood for puzzles. "Age increases your ambiguity, Mother."

"Poor girl. Surely you can't be that naïve and gullible? He's too smart to rush you. And now he has you too concerned about yourself to wonder about him. Sly fox will undoubtedly wait for eager hound to pursue. And forgive me, dear, but you have all the unmistakable symptoms of a bitch about to give tongue-scent in the field."

"Well, I wish your granddaughter could have heard that! It might alter her image of Stone Age Grandma."

"Oh, I doubt it would shock her, some of the purple language she uses! But sometimes a large dose of truth serum is the best treatment for your kind of female complaint, Lanie. I think the whole problem is that you've suddenly come alive again, out of your emotional catalepsy, and are ready to grasp at any vital stimulus. He could easily have seduced you tonight, couldn't he? If he'd pressed his advantage, you'd be in the Fiesta Motel making merry right now."

"Probably," Lanie conceded. "And go ahead and smirk, if it pleases you to have the perception of a witch. Is Beth home from the movies yet?"

"She's at a slumber party, don't you remember?"

"Oh, yes. Pamela Addison."

"Laverne Hendricks, starry-eyed Madonna. Tell me, did you get around to discussing his missing ancestral links?"

"Briefly. He read some of the society's history—surprise, surprise! And, of course, you were right. The Steeles are conspicuous by their absence."

"Well, don't begrudge me, darling. You haven't lost him, I doubt if you could. He came for something, and he'll hang around until he gets it."

"I'll bet Mary's mother said the same thing about Joseph."

42

"Mary and Joseph who?"

"Mary Virgin and Joseph Carpenter. Forget it, Mother."

"You're babbling, dear. And since you didn't make love, I trust you made conversation? That you learned *something* about him?"

"Fragments. He's an investment counselor, and his wife died in a water skiing accident last summer. Make of that what you will, Mother. I'm going to bed."

"Any plans for tomorrow?"

"None."

"Don't worry, he'll devise some. But he'll let you fret awhile. You may not hear from him for a day or two. He may even disappear temporarily."

"Until the next full moon?" Lanie sighed her impatience and disgust. "You make him sound like a werewolf, Mother. Will you be terribly disappointed if he turns out to be just an ordinary human creature?"

"Oh, I hope he won't be too ordinary," Eunice said with a meaningful smile. "But human enough to humanize you again. God knows you've been a non-person for too long."

Lanie faked a trumpet. "Well, prepare for another revelation! The Second Coming of Lanine Whitney Hall. She was dead and has risen and now wants to live, live, live! Goodnight, Mother. Fantastic dreams."

Her own were restless, frenetic. She had no appetite for breakfast and camped near the telephone all day. By the time he finally called, late that evening, Lanie was ready to send up smoke signals.

"Do you know the time, Ken?"

"Why yes, I think so. Ten o'clock. I'm sorry, Lanie. I meant to call earlier but got absorbed in my homework. Fascinating, this regional history. Still no leads, however. I went to the cemetery again and read every tombstone. Some are badly marred, the inscriptions hardly legible. Others are missing, removed for some reason if they ever existed. It's possible a couple may have marked Steele plots, but I don't know how it could be proved now. Wouldn't be anything but bones and dust left, anyway," he lamented: "This is moist earth, and a wood coffin would deteriorate rapidly. Have they ever disinterred any graves there?"

"Not to my knowledge. People are leary of disturbing the dead here, even in potter's field."

"You mean that briar patch on the other side of the fence? I thought that was unconsecrated ground, reserved for felons, reprobates and suicides to rest in ignominious anonymity."

"A few, long ago, since it was also the local boot hill in frontier times."

"So maybe the old boy was an outlaw or horse thief, hanged, shot, or exiled."

Lanie laughed. "In that case, he'd be a county legend, famous for his infamy, and the Chamber of Commerce would be capitalizing on it. No, potter's field is for paupers now. No monuments because the taxpayers would have to erect them."

Brief silence hummed on the wire. "It seems I've reached a dead end. Perhaps I should move on, to those other places you mentioned with 'wood' prefixes. Would you be good enough to direct me? Sort of weird entertainment, I realize, but you understand?"

"I'm trying," she said. "But I hope this won't become an obsession, Ken?"

"Echoes of Mom? After all, some of the founding fathers of Woodland were traced back ten generations. Surely she'll allow me to recede three or four?"

"I don't mouth Mother in everything I say, Ken. Occasionally I do have an original thought."

"And you think I'm getting morbidly obsessive on the subject? That may well be, Lanie. So if you'd prefer, just forget it. I can go alone. I have maps."

"No, please," she relented, "I want to help all I can. Woodglade is about fifty miles south of here, on the Gulf Coast. Would you like to try there next?"

"Thanks. With your help, I can check the registers, the cemeteries, and be back by nightfall. I'll make Woodland my base of operations. See you early tomorrow, Lanie."

Replacing the receiver, Lanie told her mother, "We're going to Woodglade in the morning."

"Yes, I couldn't help overhearing."

"Which proves you don't need a hearing aid."

"I must say he seems dedicated and persistent in his pursuit," Eunice observed. "I presume he's going to camp in our area awhile?"

"There you go with your possessive pronouns again!" Lanie said furiously. "Our town, our area, et cetera. You should rid yourself of these proprietary airs, Mother. We do not own Texas, you know. And he is not 'camping' in our woods, either. He's paying for his accommodations at a motel."

"He is also establishing what, I believe, in the military is called a beachhead from which to pursue the target. Was he in the service?"

"I don't know. Why don't you ask him when he comes?"

"I'll be busy at church all day, setting up booths. He's your catch, Lanine, or vice versa. But I don't think he's any great prize. You could probably do better in the charity bazaar fishpond."

"Or a box of Crackerjack?"

"You said it, dear, not I."

CHAPTER FOUR

Woodglade. An abandoned seaport at the muddy mouth of a sluggish bayou on the Mexican Gulf. Ships no longer called at the silt-filled harbor, and its dreams of becoming a metropolis had long since vanished. A few shrimp boats comprised its fleet. Some delapidated motels and cabins catered to vacationers too poor to patronize the better coastal resorts.

Neither the birth nor death records of the town revealed any Steeles, and a stroll through the only cemetery proved equally fruitless and frustrating.

"Another impasse," Ken said.

"A ghost town," Lanie said. "Sad, when you think of its great expectations. I'm sorry, Ken. This isn't much of a vacation for you."

"I didn't expect it to be, Lanie. For one thing, it's too soon after . . . too soon for a holiday. And maybe I'm just fooling myself with this project, anyway. Using it as an excuse to escape New Orleans and myself. And failing, because you can't escape self-imprisonment."

"I know," Lanie nodded. "The doctors used to advise me to get away, go on a long trip, take an ocean cruise. All the old panaceas which don't work, because you can't leave memory behind.

47

They'd say, find a new interest, don't be idle, keep busy—also ineffective, because you can't chase gloom from a mind that harbors it like cobwebs in an attic. I spent a year in analysis getting rid of mine. At least I think they're gone."

"But you're not sure?"

"Fairly sure. More so than my mother, anyway."

Driving away from the dreary solitude of damp stone and rank shrubbery, through the dead town mourned by weeping willows, Ken said, "For your sake, I hope it's not just a remission, Lanie. My chimeras disappear temporarily too, but they invariably return. I doubt it's possible to banish them completely. All we can do is try."

They came upon a dismal, debris-littered shore lapped by a murky sea. The kind of scene, Lanie knew, would depress and disturb her daughter, especially if the off-shore drilling activity responsible for the oil slick happened to be one of the myriad financial ventures of Hall industries.

Ken frowned. "Sort of takes the romance out of the sea, doesn't it?"

"That rig out there?"

"The mess it creates. We have them off the Louisana coast, too. I was going to suggest walking on the beach barefoot, wading in the surf—"

"Well, thanks. I was beginning to wonder."

"About what?"

"Myself. What you thought of me."

"If I found you attractive? Come now, you're fishing. You must know you're a beautiful and desirable woman?"

"Then why haven't you gotten physical? You haven't even kissed me."

Her hand rested on the console between the bucket seats, and he covered it with his. "I'm not sure I want to torture myself that way, Lanie. We're not kids, you know. I want to make love to you, but not with a floor-shift between us. I want the whole bit, in bed. There hasn't been anyone since—well, not for some time."

"Not for lack of opportunity, surely?"

"No, lack of interest. I loved Michele very much. I never met anyone who attracted me that way until you."

Now his hand progressed up her arm to her throat, where his fingers performed a sensuous stroking ritual. For the first time in over a year Lanie thought seriously of sex, actually longed for it. "I could make the same statement, Ken."

"But you're afraid it'd sound like a declaration, and you're not ready to commit yourself?"

Lanie was pulling apart a crimson rose she had picked at random from someone's grave; the petals lay in her lap like red teardrops. "I don't honestly know, Ken. Maybe it's too soon to know. And I've been a little mixed up since we met."

"And Mother hasn't helped, has she? Only confused you more. What does she think, Lanie—that this is a sinister scheme to get to your fortune? That I'm an adventurer, or worse? I guess I can't blame her. Why should she trust me? Why should you or anyone else, for that matter? I have no gilt-edged credentials or references."

"You don't need any with me, Ken. And be patient with Mother—she'll acquiesce eventually. She just has a mental block about our meeting ground. Thinks a cemetery is an unlikely spot for Cupid to shoot an arrow."

Gulls and sandpipers scavenged the beach, fighting over the meager booty. He seemed unaware of them, concentrating on the waves crashing against the ballast breakers in the bay, or the ship streaming on the far horizon. "On the contrary," he said moodily, "probably as many lonely hearts meet there as any other place. Indeed they gravitate in mutual loss and loneliness. Your mother's not very realistic, Lanie."

"No one could accuse Mother of realism," Lanie agreed. "She's terribly narrow in some ways, in fact. She hasn't traveled widely, because Dad couldn't leave his practice any length of time—one of those dedicated GP's virtually extinct nowadays. Her friends are people she has known all her life, and she doesn't cultivate newcomers or strangers. It's a rut, to be sure, but she's comfortable in it, happy and content. That's her privilege. But it needn't affect us, Ken. She can't control our emotions, can she? As you said, we're not kids. She can't even control her grandchild, although she tries. But Beth bucks her like a bronc."

"Guts, that kid."

"Inherited from her father, I suppose," Lanie reflected. "I'm afraid I don't have much of my own." She waited for him to dispute this, but his silence only seemed to concur. "Do you want to try another town, Ken? It's still early, and Woodbine is in this general area, toward Houston."

"No, I've had it for today, Lanie. But before we start back, I'd like to settle a more important direction. Do we go to your place or mine?"

"Yours," she said without preamble.

"It's a motel, Lanie. Wouldn't it be nicer and more private at your place?"

"The Hall Estate? I didn't know you knew—"

A gull wheeled before the windshield, diving as if it would attack. Ken started the motor. "I was driving around yesterday. Couldn't see the house for the trees, but the signs were explicit. POSTED. PRIVATE PROPERTY. NO TRESPASS-ING. KEEP OUT. VIOLATORS WILL BE PROSECUTED TO THE FULL EXTENT OF THE LAW. Not so friendly, some of you Texans. Is there an electrically charged fence and pack of vicious dogs?"

"No, just a caretaker to prevent vandalism. Don't you protect your Ponchartrain property?"

"Only by insurance. And sometimes I wish a fire or hurricane would destroy it."

"One less ghost? I know the feeling, Ken. The motel, please."

A woman couldn't ask for a better lover, from the taking off of garments to the laying on of hands; and it was a mutual seduction, equally aggressive, urgent, fulfilling. If a more level head prevailed, it was surely his, inquiring at the peak of intensity if she were safe, taking an affirmative response for granted.

"Safe?" she asked.

"On the pill?"

"No," she murmured.

"Oh, God. Then I have to interrupt this beautiful thing, and it's going to damn near kill me."

Lanie loved him for that. Few men were so considerate in the throes of passion. Brian had impregnated her on the honeymoon, possibly the wedding night. In gratitude, she held Ken so tightly he had to wrench himself free at the crucial climax.

"If I forgot to say it, Lanie, I love you."

"You didn't forget, darling. You said it beautifully, in many ways. Did I tell you?"

51

"I think so, but I was pretty busy there at the last. I hope your clinging delirium was rapture?"

"Love," she said, "and I'm deliciously happy."

"Happiness is a pair of contented lovers."

"In a motel named Fiesta." She chuckled. "Believe it or not, this is a first for me, Ken. I've never been in a situation like this before."

"Not even with Brian?"

"Not before marriage. We were just kids and pretty conventional. Oh, we toyed with the motel idea plenty, but fear of consequences is usually the great deterrent of youth. I was terrified of pregnancy—still am, in fact. And there was no pill then, of course, and the other precautions were either too messy or too risky."

"They still are, darling. Risky. But I tried."

She smiled, stroking his shoulder. "How long were you married, Ken?"

"To Michele? Seven years."

A sudden chill swept her, as if a draft had blown over her naked body. "You had other wives?"

"One other. Dorene. That lasted three years."

Lanie lay still, pondering the ceiling. The room was semidark with drawn drapes, but the partially opened bath door admitted enough light to cast shadows on the walls and into the corners. "Death?" she asked tensely.

"Divorce."

"Why didn't you tell me about Dorene the other night, Ken, when we were getting acquainted?"

"I didn't consider it important, Lanie. That was thirteen years ago, and Dorene means nothing to me now. It's as if she never existed at all—sometimes I have difficulty remembering how she looked. I was twenty-three, a shavetail stationed at Fort

Dix, New Jersey, when we met and thought it was love. The marriage didn't take, so we split."

"And no children from either union?"

"No. Dorene didn't want any, and Michele couldn't get pregnant. She was considering a fertility drug when the accident happened. Does it matter about Dorene?"

"Not really," Lanie lied. "There's just so much about you I don't know, and I want to know everything."

He touched her left breast, indenting the nipple. "In due time, dear heart. There's a lot I don't know about you, either. But what more do we need to know right now, except that we're in love? What's more important than that, Lanie?"

"Nothing, I guess."

"You sound dubious?"

Hesitating, "I—I just don't know where all this is leading, Ken."

"Where do you want it to lead?"

"Well, beyond bed, maybe. I mean, I don't make a habit of this sort of thing, Ken." She covered herself with the sheet, suddenly embarrassed. "It was incredibly easy, wasn't it? Were they so easy —Dorene and Michele?"

"Lanie." He tried to remove the sheet; she clutched at it fiercely. "What's the matter with you?"

"I want to go home, Ken."

"Run to Mommy and confess you've been a naughty girl?"

"Stop it!" She scorned his embrace and slipped out of bed, gathering up her scattered garments. "If you must know, I feel like a tramp."

"Oh, for God's sake! We made love and we both

wanted to, didn't we? Come back here, we'll talk about it."

"I'd rather not, Ken."

He was on his feet, confronting her. "Shall I use force? I warn you, I can be violent."

"I don't doubt that. And if you want to rape me, go ahead. I'll leave later."

He looked at her, bewildered, and then broke into laughter. "Our first quarrel. Natural enough for lovers, but I'm sorry it came so soon. Forgive me, darling."

"Get dressed," Lanie said, averting her eyes, and as he proceeded, "What is it with us, Ken? I'm not sure. It all happened so fast. Three days ago we didn't even know each other, and here we are fighting in a motel. Is that your usual way with women?"

"Well, goddamn," he muttered. "I thought it was something special, Lanie. You're the one trying to make it seem like something else now. But don't worry, it won't happen again. I'm leaving tomorrow."

"And you wanted one for the road, is that it?"

"Lanie, I'm not retired. I have a business to run. Unfortunately my resources are not as limitless as yours."

"What about the big ancestor hunt?"

"It's getting expensive, and I'm probably in the wrong territory," he said. "But I'm not broke, and I'm not a vagabond lover. I can stay longer if you want me to, Lanie."

"Don't do me any favors," she said and immediately apologized. "Sorry—that was bitchy, but saving that departure news until after the fact was sort of bastardly." She waited, and he nodded agreement. "Are you paying alimony to Dorene?"

"No, she waived it."

"Where is she now?"

Shrugging, he said, "I don't know. Probably in that same Trenton underwear factory, sewing labels on girdles and bras. She went home to New Jersey after the divorce, and I haven't seen or heard from her since."

"Was her family poor?"

"Ghetto dwellers, practically on welfare."

"And Michele's?"

"Loaded, and as aristocratic as they come in this country. I was as out of my class with Michele as I am with you." Partially dressed, he paused to light a cigarette. "My father was a stevedore. My mother sews Mardi Gras costumes in a French Quarter shop. I was born in the Irish Channel, which is the worst slum in New Orleans. I had a kid sister who died at six of polio. I worked to put myself through college, served my military hitch, married Dorene Granato, was divorced three years later. I managed to get a position with Peter Danielle, married his daughter—and you know the rest. That's a fairly accurate résumé, Lanie, but I'll furnish details if you insist."

Appeased somewhat, Lanie relented. "Don't be angry with me, Ken. I'm interested, is all. And jealous of the other women in your life. Is that so terrible?"

"No, but there are no others now, Lanie. Only you."

She smiled at him in the mirror, where she stood fixing her face and hair, curious in spite of herself about the others. Were they pretty, dark, fair?

He was watching her, smoking and brooding, apparently reading her mind. "They were both brunettes," he said.

"I wasn't thinking—"

"Weren't you? Michele was tanned from outdoor sports, and Dorene was a mixture of Italian and Jew, although she denied the latter. Idiot, ashamed of her blood."

"Then a blond should be a novelty for you?" She bit her tongue, expecting reprisal. It came.

"Oh, I've known a few blonds, baby. Just never married one . . . yet."

"I deserved that."

"Yes, you did."

Chastised, Lanie said, "I'm ready to go now. And, Ken—there's no reason for you to continue staying here, in this motel."

"I should be a guest in your mother's home, maybe?"

"No, in mine. There're some twenty rooms, all vacant, and the utilities on. The caretaker has his own quarters. You'd be more comfortable there, and doing the estate a favor. Vacancy insurance is exorbitant."

"I don't know what to say, Lanie."

"Yes is a good response, isn't it?"

"Yes," he said.

CHAPTER FIVE

As Lanie had expected, her mother hit the twelve-foot ceiling of Whitney House.

"I can't believe it, Lanine. I simply cannot believe you have turned the estate over to Kenneth Steele!"

"Not the deed, Mother, just a key to the house. And only temporarily, for the remainder of his vacation. Why not? What harm can he possibly do? You can't hurt a house."

"But, darling, you know nothing about this man, except what he has deigned to tell you, which may or may not be true. You're impetuous to say the least."

"Mother, I'm not a child. I'm thirty-five years old, and I think I'm capable of making a few value judgments for myself. If they're wrong, I'll take the blame and consequences, not you. So please stop telling me what to do. If you must pass down your wisdom and offer your guidance, concentrate on your granddaughter."

"That recalcitrant child! It's like trying to chip granite."

"Well, keep chiseling away, and eventually you might sculpture her to the desired form and specifications. Frankly, I've given up and gladly pass the Pymalion project to you."

"At the moment, I'm more concerned about your image," Mrs. Whitney said. "Exactly how serious is this thing between you and Steele?"

Lanie waxed wistful. "I think I'm in love with him."

"Oh, don't be sentimental idiot! You're being beguiled and exploited. Is sex involved?"

"That's my business," Lanie snapped.

"And that answers my question. You've been to bed with him. I don't know whether you've lost your heart or your head, Lanie, and if you marry Kenneth Steele I won't know whether to congratulate or commit you."

"Then you might as well start proceedings, Mother. Because I'm considering marriage."

Eunice began to pace the carpet, trying to suppress her irritation. "Here I've been worrying about Beth losing her balance, while you were losing your common sense. Is it possible you are pregnant?"

"I hope not."

"Don't tell me you let him take the precaution! The oldest trap in the world and you stumbled obligingly into it. But it needn't work for Mr. Clever. The baby-trap is fairly easy to spring now."

For a sheltered matron, her sophistication was sometimes startling. "Well, the square-cut stone has some brilliant facets, after all! But shall we wait awhile—like a month or so—before flying off to an abortionist?"

"I just hope and pray you won't regret your abandon in more ways than one, Lanine. And now that he's possessed you, when does he take possession of your property?"

"I'm going there now to welcome him."

58

"He'll be there forever, you know. The rest of his life, or yours, whichever come first."

Lanie smiled, humoring her. "You're reading a new Gothic novel, right? So how do you visualize Kenneth Steele now? Bluebeard, Svengali? I assure you, he didn't hypnotize me, Mother. I'm acting entirely on my own volition. This invitation was strictly my idea, and it humbled him."

"Indeed? And do you plan to live together in humility, without benefit of clergy or convention?"

"Not unless you throw me out."

"That would be rather like tossing the rabbit to the wolf, wouldn't it?"

"Grandma, what a big imagination you have! But I'm not Little Red Riding Hood."

"No, you're even more naïve, Lanine. But it's your life and perhaps I've interfered enough."

"I agree," Lanine said on her way out.

For a realistic man, Brian Tyson Hall had erected an unrealistic residence. The previous family homestead, built in an era of architectural flamboyance, had been pretentious enough with its grotesque gables and gaudy ornamentations, replacing the former tasteful white frame mansion that had replaced the original log cabin, the dwellings progressing dimensionally with fortune. But this palace in the pines had no precedent. All other structures had been leveled to accommodate it. The design was difficult to describe. East Indian in some respects, and verging on the monumental. It had occasioned some curiosity, comment, and criticism during construction; but the consensus seemed to be that kings must indulge their whims and fancies, and Brian Tyson Hall had been the undisputed monarch of Lower East Texas.

A maintenance crew labored on the grounds, which were terraced and landscaped like a private park. There were reflecting pools and sparkling fountains, a boxwood maze and sunken rose garden. The caretaker, Lemil Furbusher, occupied a comfortable apartment above the eight-car garage. Inherently churlish, he was disgruntled when informed there would be a guest in residence. Furbusher himself never entered the manor except on duty or rare invitation and then only via the servants' entrance.

"Will the staff be returning, ma'am?"

"I'm not sure yet," Lanie replied. "Not all, at any rate. Depends on Mr. Steele's wishes. As I said, his stay is only temporary. But please help him all you can."

"Yes, ma'am."

"And, Lem, don't brandish your rifle around. It's unnecessary to patrol the premises like an armed guard. There hasn't been a prowler or trespasser in months, has there?"

"None I seen or heard, ma'am."

"You're a good watchman, Lem. But I think you can relax your vigilance now. Pay more attention to general duties."

"Whatever you say, ma'am."

Lanie proceeded through the imposing entrance somewhat reluctantly, trying to reconcile her reason for leaving a year ago with the one for returning today. The visual impact was always startling, and she still thought the interior decorators had gone a little berserk. Too many tapestries and Oriental carpets, too much velvet and damask, crystal and porcelain and bronze, riches piled on riches, as if a caravan of royal contraband had fallen into their hands and they weren't quite sure

60

how to dispose of it. Grandeur on a massive scale, but little intimacy, coziness, or reflection of individual personalities. Impersonal enough together, challenging alone. Actually they had been happiest away from the overwhelming mansion and it accounted for their frequent travels. Lanie had also accompanied her husband on many of his business trips, but had been grounded by flu on the fatal flight.

Now there was someone else. Someone who could be more than a substitute. And it was hysterical of her mother to impute sinister motives to his interest, and insane ones to her own. Suspicious soul, she never completely trusted anyone at whose birth a Whitney physician had not officiated.

Cleaned regularly, pantries and freezers perennially stocked, temperature seasonally controlled, the house was always ready for occupancy. Lanie had only to select a welcoming bottle of champagne from the well-provisioned wine cellar. Whatever luxury the stevedore's son had acquired through associaiton with Peter Danielle's daughter, she was confident it could not compare, much less surpass, that which Brian Hall's widow could provide. Not that she believed material inducements were necessary to their relationship, but why not employ every advantage?

And Ken was properly impressed. Awed, in fact, as if he'd entered an alien temple and was uncertain of the prescribed ritual. "My God," he murmured reverently. "Do I bow, kneel, or genuflect? I don't know what I expected, Lanie, but not this. This is too much."

"Be it ever so humble," she shrugged.

"Is the floor plan posted somewhere? I might get lost and wander for days."

Lanie was not amused, and she actually resented humor directed at herself or possessions. "I have some champagne on ice," she said coolly.

Shunning Furbusher's assistance, Ken had carried in two pieces of luggage, a battered flight bag with bulging side pockets, and a dark-Dacron extra suit in a plastic garment bag. "How did the Big Bertha react to this maneuver? Any flak?"

"Forget Mother, Ken. I'm mistress of this house."

"More like the chatelaine of a castle, I'd say. Pray assign this humble wayfarer a room."

"Take your choice," she invited.

"I'd rather you made the selection."

"As long as it's not his? We shared the master suite, Ken. It's the largest and most sybaritic, but I have no objection to your using it."

"I'd prefer a guest room, Lanie. That's my status here, isn't it? And I'll try not to abuse the privilege."

"Don't be so damned cynical!" Why did he have to spoil her pleasure in giving? Had there been too many female gifts, with or without strings attached? Did he actually resent such feminine favors while unable to resist them? Some dimensions of his personality defied and eluded her, but she had no desire just then to try to define and explore them. "I planned a happy welcome, Ken, and you might be more cooperative."

"You mean appreciative? Sorry. It's just that I'm not accustomed to such gratuities. I usually earn way, Lanie. I'm not a gigolo."

"Nobody is accusing you of that, Ken. But sometimes you seem to act and speak with a guilty conscience." She paused to smile reassuringly at him, apologizing for her petulance. "The servants have been dismissed, but I could rehire them. A maid and cook, anyway."

"No, please. I can manage alone, and I'd rather. It won't be for long." He watched her spinning the bottle in an ornate silver cooler. "I've finished the regional history, Lanie. Interesting, all of it, and especially the Big Thicket. I'd like to see more of it. One of the chroniclers described it as a last true frontier and barrier against civilization. No wonder it intrigues your daughter. It must seem like Eden incarnate to the young ecologists."

"The Thicket's a jungle, Ken, not a paradise. Swamps, poisonous snakes, wild animals, impenetrable growth. Stray a hundred yards off the main road alone, and the sheriff would have to use bloodhounds to find you."

"But people do live there?"

"Indians on the reservation in the northern part. A few hearty descendants of pioneers who tried to settle it, and assorted hermits and recluses. But most of the towns that sprang up with the lumber and oil operations are ghosts now, and it's about as uncivilized a wilderness as you'll find west of the Mississippi."

"Maybe. But some of the Louisiana bayou country is pretty wild, too."

"Listen to me, Ken. Experienced hunters have gotten lost and died in the Big Thicket. It's been a haven for renegades, outlaws, and Army deserters since the Civil War, when a group of Jayhawkers actually had to be burned out. During Prohibition there were stills that the Revenue agents could never locate, and a few regretted trying. Game wardens risk their lives with poachers. Wanderers have disappeared without a trace. Murder, rape, and other crimes have been committed there without detection and the culprits never apprehended. If you decide to explore it and value your life, hire a native guide. And while we're on the subject, please don't mention your avid interest to my daughter. She's forbidden to go into the Thicket. It's no place for a stranger, and certainly not for a naïve young girl."

"Well, I'm not in the habit of luring naïve young girls into the bushes, my dear. And I can't remember ever having lost one that way."

"I didn't mean that, exactly."

"What did you mean, exactly?"

"Just don't encourage Beth's independence too much," Lanie said, removing the frosted bottle of Dom Perignon. "I think this is ready—will you do the honors?"

"Is it customary for a guest?"

"Consider yourself host."

Host, not master; the distinction was clear enough, and any experienced traveler knew the difference. A head waiter could be a host. A wine steward could be a host.

"Of course," he bowed and slipped the cork from the bottle, since any connoisseur knew it wasn't supposed to be popped like a firecracker.

CHAPTER SIX

Watching the rider's spirited approach, Ken was reminded of another expert equestrienne. But Michele had used a regulation saddle, and this girl was bareback, wearing the same Indian regalia in which he had first met her, long dark braids fluttering, mouth so naturally vivid it might have been stained with wild berry juice. The sight fairly delighted him, for he wanted very much for this uninhibited child to like him. He had the door open before she dismounted and ran up the walk on feet as fleet as the stallion's.

"Greetings," he said warily, like a squatter expecting eviction. Co-owner of the property, she might challenge or revoke his temporary trespasser's permit.

"Relax, man. I come in peace. Don't you recognize the sign? One-horse welcome wagon, that's me. Somebody might as well get some use out of the place, since Mom won't turn it over to charity. You ever see such a sinful waste of bread? If Dad wasn't so straight, I'd swear he was freaked out when he conceived this massive monstrosity. Walt Disney couldn't have dreamed up a greater fantasyland."

"It's something, all right."

"Something else," Beth muttered, sprawling on one of the twin gold velvet sofas in the opulent living room. "You sort of expect to find a throne and stage for court jesters, don't you? Once, when I was at the fairytale age, I invited a poor friend to visit me, and she imagined my parents were the King and Queen of Texas. I thought so myself, because Daddy always called me his little princess. Maybe he was trying to preserve a legend—you know, the fabulous Texan? And Mom humored him. This just couldn't be her idea—anybody's idea—of a real home. No wonder she split so soon after the state funeral. Imagine trying to be cozy here alone?" She trained crystal-gray eyes on Ken, like laser beams to penetrate his character. "You and Her Majesty hung up romantically?"

"You'd better ask her that," Ken said.

"I did. Got the old runaround routine. Mom went to a fancy finishing school, where her best subjects were Evasion and Procrastination. So I decided to study you myself, in case you're going to be my new daddy. Are you?"

"You shoot from the hip, don't you?"

"It's the best way, man. Are you dodging me?"

"Only because I don't know the answer, Beth. But would you approve if things developed that way?"

Another horse-trader appraisal. "I might. You don't seem too square, or out of it. Some of those other creeps that tried to get to Mom—ugh!"

"If that's a compliment, thanks. But I'm not trying to get your mother, Beth."

"Hah! I bet you already have, man, one way or another." She jumped up as if spring levered. "Pardon me Señor. It's tinkle time in fantasyland."

She retreated to her private facilities. Her suite

was just as she'd left it, redecorated at various stages of her growth, but still essentially a royal nursery. God, how she'd hated the corny Princess Period of pink and white ruffles, as if she were a bonbon in a fluted cup, with a cream-filled brain! Dainty clothes, hair ribbons, slippers with bows on the toes. Silk pajamas sprinkled with rosebuds. Stuffy stories about impossible characters and situations, when she wanted to read about real people and places, about Life and Love and Sex. And so had to do it in secret, borrowing books from her less-censored friends, sometimes paying out of her generous allowance for the privilege; and sneaking off on her horse to study nature, hunt for arrowheads in the woods, or just be alone to think, wonder, dream, hope, plan. Her father had indulged her, perhaps to compensate for mother's stringency, and then one day he was gone, her mother was sick under her grandmother's care, their vigilance was relaxed, and she was finally free. Like being released from a gilded cage, and she was determined never to go back into it. She would fight anyone who tried to make her.

A curious check of the master chambers showed no signs of habitation. Her mother's scruples, or Mr. Steele's? Why did Grandma resent him so much, when she didn't even know him? But of course that was why: she didn't know him or his family, and she was suspicious of strangers.

"Taking inventory, princess?" he asked when she returned. "Call in the guard if you have any doubts, but I assure you nothing's missing, except some choice liquor." He was at the bar, sampling the private stock. "Your daddy was a connoisseur, and your mommy told me to help myself. But I'm not a thief."

"What are you, Mr. Steele?"

"Just a man. Ordinary homo sapiens variety."

Beth removed a coke from the refrigerator, popped the cap. "Most homo sapiens of your vintage are saps. But Mom seems to consider you special enough for this museum. Grandma thinks she's out of her skull, but Grandma grooves on genealogy. She's pure WASP and has a hard sting."

"Yeah, I've met her stinger."

"Well, you couldn't have used a worst pitch with Grandma, man. A person's background is his bond with her, and you came out of the woods supposedly hunting your family tree."

"Not supposedly, Beth."

"No matter," she shrugged. "I couldn't care less if you came out of the sea or space. But don't expect Grandma to feel that same way. She knows the origins of every human being on this part of the planet. And voting the Democratic ticket is about as liberal as she gets. The past is where it's at for Grandma, and you may not be able to make that scene to her satisfaction."

"Did Grandma tell you all this?"

"I had my antenna up when she was rapping with Mom."

"And concluded that I'm an imposter?"

"I didn't say that, and I don't always agree with Grandma. Rarely, in fact. And right now I've got my own tug of war going with her." She leaned forward confidentially, elbows propped on the marble bar counter, chin in hands, bare feet hooked around the luxuriously padded stool. "How're you at secrets, man?"

"Secretive."

"Well, I'll trust you, because I have to tell someone, or bust. Last spring I met an Indian on the reservation in the Big Thicket. Our school made its annual field trip, and he was the guide for our class. It's a big tourist deal, you know. Museum and shops, tribal dances and food and tours in the forest. Not many Indians left in Texas—only the two tribes in the Thicket and some Tequas in El Paso. Grandma's all for the reservation and is on some committees that support it. The Indians are a part of our heritage, you see, and she thinks every white kid should be able to see a Real Live Indian. Some noble incentive, huh?"

Ken swirled the twelve-year-old Scotch in his glass. "Remnants of slavery are preserved elsewhere in the South for similar 'noble' reasons," he said. "But what's the secret, Beth. Have you been seeing this brave on the sly?"

"A few times," she admitted.

"What's his name?"

"Mark Carradine."

"Mark?"

"You expected Geronimo or something? Oh, he has an Indian name, too. Little Wolf. His father was Big Wolf, and his grandfather is Wise Wolf. And Mark can speak the language—they all learn their tongue before ours, because they take their heritage seriously. It's not just a tourist gimmick to them, and they must get awfully tired of the cornballs asking dumb questions and staring at them. What do they expect—painted savages in breechcloths leaping out from behind trees waving tomahawks and bloody scalps!"

"Probably," Ken said. "This way they expect every old Southern plantation to be Tara."

"Well, Mark's a Christian, named for the apostle, and baptized in the Presbyterian Mission Church on the reservation. And he knows Scripture much better than I, because I goofed off in Sunday School and our minister's sermons bore me. Mark lives in a frame house built by his grandfather years ago— the tepees are for the tourists. The house is small, only three rooms and needs repairs and furniture, which they can't afford. His parents are dead. Firewater and frustration killed his father before he was forty, and tuberculosis took his mother. The village used to be plagued with disease. They have nurses and medical care now, and it's healthier."

"But still a reservation?"

"Yes, with two chiefs, and a tribal council. But not self-supporting yet. Some of the Indians work in the local fields and forests and industries. My father employed numbers of them, and I could probably arrange a good job for Mark now—but he's going to college on an athletic scholarship this fall. Basketball and track. Indians are terrific jumpers and runners, you know, and good at competitive sports. Maybe because just living is an endless competition for them."

Her interest seemed genuine. "Sounds like Mark Carradine might have some future," Ken said.

"He doesn't think so," Beth frowned, "and I can't convince him. He says no full-blooded Indian can make it big in the white world, all he can do is survive. Nobody tells a little Indian boy he might grow up to be president someday. But Mark Carradine would be, if one vote could elect him."

"How old is he?" Ken asked.

"Nineteen. And he doesn't look Indian, except maybe his black hair, black eyes, and high cheekbones."

Ken smiled. "Except his face, you mean."

"Anyway, his skin's not red. It's bronze, like the Aztecs who worshipped the sun. And clear and smooth, because adolescent Indians don't usually have acne. Mark's the best-looking boy I know. Would you like to meet him, Ken?"

"Sure, if I'm around long enough."

Beth toyed with her coke, shaking the bottle to make it fizz, watching the bubbles explode. "It's not right, you know. Mark's ancesters were one of the mighty Creek Nations, and all this land was theirs even before the Spanish and French and Mexicans claimed it. Now they're confined to four thousand acres in the Big Thicket, like rare animals on a preserve."

"Things change, Beth, or stagnate. Most change is considered progress."

"Progress for who? The white man. The other races here haven't had much of it, and the Indian least of all. There's not enough of them left to be a political force, to impress the Big White Father in the Big White Hut in Washington! If I were an Indian, I think I'd be out raiding white settlements right now, demanding the land, lumber, cattle, horses, oil, minerals—everything that was taken or stolen from me. Do I sound like a firebrand?"

"A torch is a torch, no matter who carries it," Ken said. "Pocahontas for Captain Smith, or Beth Hall for Mark Carradine. Don't you see, honey? You're all afire about one Indian, not the whole race. And you want to get your friend off the reservation, not share it with him. There's a difference between caring and crusading, Beth. Don't confuse them."

"What are you, psychic? How do you know what I think and feel and want? Anyway, I didn't come here for advice. I came to get acquainted. Maybe I wasted my time. I'm not so sure I want to know you. Not sure I like you living in my father's house and lapping up his booze, either. Grandma may have some blind spots in her vision, but maybe she sees through you clear enough. Maybe it's Mom who's myopic."

Ken's glass was sweating, dampening his hands. "I didn't just wander in here like some gypsy and set up camp, Beth. I was invited."

"Not by me!"

"Suppose you just get on your horse, miss, and ride off into the sunset?"

"It's still morning, or don't you know the time of day? And what're you grinning about? You think I'm funny?"

"I think you need some discipline, and I just might be a candidate for the job. How does a premature spanking appeal to you, baby?"

"Screw you." Beth slipped easily off the stool and glared her fury and defiance. "My hail and farewell sentiments, sir. Screw you."

Ken laughed. "Did that make you feel better?"

"It's honest."

"So's a bowel movement, young lady, but it's not nice in public." He followed her outside, reluctant to part on those terms. "I'm sorry you resent and reject me, Beth. I'd hoped we could be friends. I need an ally."

"In your campaign to win Mom?" They'd reached the Appaloosa cropping the green velvet lawn. "Why should I help you in that? Maybe I don't want a goddamn stepfather."

"Then you're going to fight me?"

"I don't make deliberate war on anyone," Beth replied, mounting. "But it's hard to remain neutral in something that could affect my whole life."

"I understand," Ken nodded, smiling up at her, an

ingratiating grin almost as effective as Mark's.
"Truce?"

Relenting slightly, "Well, okay—but I'm not
promising anything, man," and pivoting and spur-
ring Brute, she thundered off like a miniature tor-
nado.

"Frisky little filly," the caretaker remarked, ap-
pearing like a weasel from the shrubbery. "Needs
a curbed bit."

Was he a self-appointed spy, Ken wondered, or
acting on instructions? And if so, whose and why?

"The spirit of youth," Ken drawled. "She's endowed with it, in more ways than one."

"Spoiled brat." Furbusher spat into the turf.
"Apple of her daddy's eye, and he didn't let her
want for nothing. A Shetland pony when she was
two years old, an Arabian mare at six, and that
Appaloosa stallion for her tenth birthday, letting
her chose from a string of thoroughbreds paraded
before her. Never mind the cost, just make his
Little Princess happy. Her ma and grandma had
fits, thinking that big brute would be too hard
for her to handle. But she was practically born in
the saddle. Her parents used to ride to hounds.
They had hunt parties and barbecues and such in
season."

"I don't see any stables or kennels?"

"The horses and dogs were brought over from
one of the Hall ranches," the caretaker explained.
"The kid's beast is kept at a local stable. But the
Queen ain't rode since the King's death, not even
in last fall's biggest hunt. Ain't done much of anything that I know of, never seen a woman so
downed by grief. But that little filly, wow! She ain't
broke to the saddle yet, not by a long shot. Ain't

gonna accept a substitute trainer easy, neither, you can bet."

"Oh, I don't know," Ken speculated. "I'd say she's eager for one without realizing it. Care for a drink, Furbusher?"

"You done said the magic word, Mr. Steele. It's hellish hot out here today. Trees bar the Gulf breezes. Say, you hear about the will?"

They were inside and at the cool oasis before Ken asked, "What about it?"

"About to clear probate, finally. All in the Houston papers this morning. Millions, the missus will get. The kid, too. Assets even the lawyers didn't seem to know about. All over the country—the world, in fact."

Putting some bottles on the bar, Ken invited the caretaker to choose his pleasure, expecting his taste to run to rye or rum. "Were you surprised by the family wealth, Furbusher? I didn't think it was a secret. Hall Industries is one of the largest corporations in North America, one of the top ten on the list."

Furbusher chose rye, filling a tumbler. "Been keeping track of it, have you?"

"That's my business," Ken said. "I'm a stock-broker."

"What firm?"

"My own."

"Well, if you're here looking for prospective clients, I can tell you these folks don't jar loose easy. Hall never left nothing to any of his servants for 'long and faithful service' like some rich people do. I worked for him seventeen years, and his pa before him, and neither of 'em left me one thin dime. Nor any of their slaves."

"What sort of man was Brian Hall?"

"The kind old timers call a rugged individualist, and young folks call something else now. Money was his god, and this temple is full of his idols. Didn't believe much in charity or philanthropy, though. Figured people should hack their own path in life and deserved only what they got for themselves, no matter how they got it. Other'n that, he was okay, I guess. Not too damn friendly, either."

"In other words, you didn't drink with him?"

"Shit!" Furbusher pursed his lips to spit, remembering he was inside. "The only way the hired help could taste his liquor was steal it."

"Well, maybe I wouldn't be so generous either, if it were mine. Since it's not, have another, man. Try the Scotch, it's twelve-year-old stuff."

"Imagine that."

"How about your helpers?"

"Them guys? The nigger wouldn't appreciate good booze, and the Injun'd go ape on firewater. They're just day workers, anyhow. No call for privileges."

Whatever information he could glean from this bitter bigot wasn't worth the effort, and Ken regretted playing the genial host to him. "Maybe I'd better make my position clear, Furbusher. I advise other people how to make money in the market, but I don't have much myself—so I wouldn't be able to do you any good, in any case. As for my social status, my father was a longshoreman on the Mississippi."

"That right? I got a brother working in a brewery in New Orleans. Ah well, we can't all be tycoons, can we?" He emptied his glass and refilled it. "Some of us can be lucky enough to inherit money, though —or marry it."

That ended the brief comaraderie, and Furbusher knew it. He stood, clapping his straw hat on his head. "Reckon I'd better get back on the job, before them dummies foul up something. Can't trust 'em on their own, and everything's got to be A-one perfect around here. Manicured lawn, symmetrical hedges—don't dare get one of them boxwoods off level. Bet you ain't seen estate grounds better tended nowhere."

The Danielle properties had been almost as well kept, but not quite. "You do a good job," Ken admitted.

"Sure, and what's my reward?"

"A salary, a place to live, a pick-up to drive. A man could do worse, Furbusher."

"A man could do better, too," the caretaker muttered, "if he was young and handsome. He could fuck his way into a fortune, right, Mr. Steele?"

Ken removed a couple of cans of beer from the bar fridge. "Give these to your boys," he said, "with my compliments. What are their names?"

"The black's Cal Sarton, and the Indian's Gray Fulton."

"How far is the Big Thicket from here?"

"Twenty miles or so. Why?"

"I just wondered."

"Anything else, sir?"

"No, that's all. Thank you."

76

"Good grief!" Mrs. Whitney exclaimed, as her granddaughter streaked through the hall on her way upstairs. "Was that an Indian, Mexican, or Mexican-Indian? It's hard to tell from her clothes and complexion."

"She thinks her tan looks natural, Mother."

"Natural for leather," Eunice said. "I wonder what she's been up to now? She acts angry or guilty about something. Where do you suppose she goes on that beast every day?"

"That beast cost seven thousand dollars, Mother. He's a thoroughbred and a beauty."

"I still don't care for Appaloosas. They're coarse animals, savage-looking."

Lanie smiled. "I think you're prejudiced because the Perce Nez Indians first introduced them, Mother. Some very horsey folks fancy them now. The palomino is passé."

"Indeed? They took most of the prizes at the last show."

"Because the judges owned most of them. Brute would win honors too, if Beth would bother to groom and train him. But you know she considers horse and dog shows the ultimate in social snobbery. Nevertheless, Brute is no cayuse."

The room where they sat was ageless, with fine woods and fine fabrics, which had made the various transitions from drawing room to parlor to living room without sacrificing elegance or dignity; a room where eyebrows might discreetly raise but no voices, and Mrs. Whitney continued calmly, "No matter, he's still too much horse for a young lady. And the wild, reckless way she rides—she'll break her neck someday."

"It's her neck," Lanie reminded.

"Is that all you can say? I declare, a form of madness has invaded this house, and I don't understand any of it. What's happening at the estate? Do you know, or don't you care? Have you spoken with him today?"

"Him has a name, Mother. Him's Kenneth, and him's not required to report daily."

"Has he abandoned his genealogical search?"

"Not altogether, but it's becoming tedious and time-consuming. He's hit so many detours and dead ends."

"On the contrary, I'd say he's precisely where he expected and intended to be, and perhaps even ahead of schedule. Have you set a date yet?"

"For what?"

"The nuptials."

"No, not yet."

"Dare I hope you're waking. Sleeping Beauty, to discover he's not a prince, after all?"

"It's just that—well, I'm afraid Beth doesn't care much for him," Lanie worried.

"Does it matter?"

"Certainly, and this morning she wanted to talk about it, I think. But I couldn't respond. And then she jogged off to the stable for Brute. She might need a father, but I'm not at all sure she wants one."

"Then you'll have to decide which is more important, her wishes or yours."

"It's not that simple, Mother. I can't just ignore my feelings or forget them. On the other hand, I couldn't do anything to deliberately alienate my child, either."

"That's the first sensible conclusion you've reached since Mr. Steele appeared on the scene," Eunice said, compressing her lips. "Maybe there's hope for you, after all."

"Hope?"

"That it's only infatuation and is fading."

Lanie rose from the damask chair. "I'll be late to the board meeting if I don't hurry. Why they want my presence is beyond me. I know nothing about corporate affairs."

"Perhaps it's time you learned?"

"Why? It's damnably boring. Conferences, consultations. Like some great legal cabala, and I don't understand the mysteries, secrets, language. I sit like a dummy, nodding when the lawyers and managers pull the strings. Consulting me is a mere formality. They'll do what they must anyway." She picked up her bag and white gloves. "If Ken calls, you know where I am. I told him yesterday, but he may have forgotten. And will you ask Maple to please press my white shantung dress and polish the pumps I wear with it?"

But half-way to the meeting, Lanie made an impulsive U-turn in the street and headed instead for the estate. It was always a pleasant drive, along densely wooded, pine-scented lanes bordered with bluebonnets in spring, Indian paintbrush and buttercups and purple verbena in summer, and wild roses most of the year.

Lanie loved it, not only because it was her native

land, but because she could relate to its idyllic, almost mystic beauty and enchantment. She and Brian could have lived anywhere in the world, but no other place had appealed to them as much. It was just too bad that the house they had built together was so formidable alone.

She imagined Ken would be outdoors strolling one of the many lateral roads, or at least enjoying the glories of the garden. Instead, admitting herself with her key, she found him brooding at the bar, nursing a partially filled glass.

"Cheers!" she greeted.

She looked mint-julep cool and crisp in jade but extremely crushable, like an exquisite doll to be handled with extreme care. He rose to embrace her, kissed her cheek lightly, as if afraid of spoiling her perfection. In contrast to her offspring's disarray, not a wisp of her carefully arrayed pale amber hair was out of order.

"Weren't you supposed to be in a conference this afternoon, Madam Chairman?"

"Playing hooky—and they'll never miss me. But that peck wasn't much of a welcome, Mr. Steele. I've had sexier kisses from little boys and old men."

"Sorry. It's the atmosphere, I guess. This place is overwhelming, Lanie. The kind of house that possesses people, not vice versa. A mere human being couldn't possibly seem important here, unless he'd designed and built it himself. And even then he'd have to be something of an egocentric and megalomaniac. It's an indomitable domain."

He haunted the bar again and Lanie pursued, tapping the bottle. "How much of this Scotch philosophy have you had so early in the day? Can't you find anything else to do? You're not a prisoner, you know. Incarcerated. You're free to come and go, as you please."

"I was hoping you'd say something else."

"Like what?"

"Like let's go to bed and find out if it's the house, or us." They hadn't yet made love there, and her discretion—or was it reluctance and evasion?—bothered him. Had he only imagined her commitment in the motel? "We haven't exactly been promiscuous since the initiation, Lanie. And maybe we couldn't make it together here? Maybe I'd be a dud—impotent—and you'd be inhibited?"

"Vulnerable, anyway," she said. "I haven't gotten my prescription yet. It's silly, but I'm embarrassed about calling Dr. Ramsey."

"Lanie, I know this is a small town, but surely you don't think the doctor would be censorious of your sex life?" His brows rose in mock horror. "What do you suppose the druggist thought when I bought the Trojans?"

"Nothing, of course. It's just me, one of my hangups. In some respects, I'm more Victorian than Mother."

"How did you handle the problem in marriage?" Lanie averted her eyes, but he touched her arm, demanding attention. "Answer me."

"I was pregnant the first nine months," she replied. "After the baby, I used a diaphragm for awhile. Then Brian had a vasectomy. And don't look so surprised. It's not mutilation or martyrdom. He knew how I felt about more children, and it's a simple procedure for a man."

"Also irreversible. Understandable with several kids, but you'd only dominoed once. And certainly economy was not a factor. Suppose there had been a divorce, or you'd died first?"

"Should I have been spayed instead? It's major surgery for a woman."

"You could have compromised," he said. "Did you love him, Lanie?"

"Of course!"

"Why 'of course' in that tone? Love is neither imperative nor synonymous in marriage, my dear. It can and does exist without it."

"The voice of experience? Did you love either of your wives, or neither?"

"I loved them both in the beginning, and Michele to the end."

"But not Numero Uno?"

He scowled. "We were divorced, Lanie. Love died, or was destroyed. Songs and poems to the contrary, it's neither eternal nor indestructible."

"Who was the first dropout—you or Dorene?"

"I think it was mutual and simultaneous. One day it was there, the next it wasn't, and we both knew it."

Lanie promptly denied any such fickleness in her union. "Well, that wasn't the case with Brian and me. We were so much in love, I didn't think I could live without him. My psychiatrist said I had a death wish, which might be suicidal, and Mother watched me like a hawk. I almost crashed mentally. Except for Beth, I might have."

"But still you had refused more children?"

He saw emotional quiverings in her breast, fluttering the crisp green fabric, and her voice rose a sharp octave. "I don't owe you any explanations for that part of life, Ken. But childbirth wasn't easy for me, and I guess I developed an innate fear of it. Furthermore, I don't see anything especially beautiful or romantic in pregnancy. I hated being misshapen and miserable, the pain of labor—the whole obscene and violent ordeal!"

His cynical gaze seemed to challenge her earlier declaration of undying love and devotion for her husband. "You may have loved Brian, Lanie, but you cheated him. No wonder he adored Beth—she was all you ever really gave him of yourself, wasn't she?"

"I didn't skip that meeting, Ken, to be amateurishly analyzed, or quarrel with you about anything. I really came to discuss my daughter."

"The floor is yours."

"I need a drink first." She dropped an olive into a crystal goblet and drowned it in vodka. "I've been trying to decide what to tell her about us, Ken. She's curious, naturally, and I'm avoiding a premature confrontation. You see, I don't believe she's either ready or willing to accept a stepfather."

"Any suggestions?"

"Just patience, darling." She dawdled with the captive olive, teasing it like a swizzle, nibbling it from the pick. "Maybe you can win her over? It shouldn't be too hard, with your charm and persuasion?"

"You want me to work at it, Lanie?"

"Not physically, dear. Psychologically."

"Don't you think the stepparent relationship evolves better when the child initiates it? A pushy adult can seem overbearing. Ordinarily—"

Lanie interrupted, "Beth isn't an ordinary child, Ken. She's different and difficult, especially since adolescence. I don't understand her myself." Puberty in her own experience had been a fairly simple and natural process, in which she was primarily concerned with developing a bust and preventing acne.

She'd had a resident physician to explain sex, and her mother had gone out and bought her her first bra, bar of medicated soap, and box of Kotex. Cigarettes were her secret vice, she'd 'freaked-out' once at a beer party, and the only wild togs she wore were to rodeos. "My girlhood was complacent and uncomplicated. I was frivolous and shallow. My mind was transparent. Beth's is a puzzle, full of complexities and anxieties, which are clouded by the current youth mystique."

"Maybe she's in love?" Ken suggested.

"At sixteen?"

"That's the most susceptible age."

"For puppy love, but Beth doesn't even go steady, or date much at all. Perhaps she needs a father image, an older man to relate to and confide in. Will you try with her, Ken?"

He frowned. "Furbusher says she's spoiled."

"The caretaker?" Her brows elevated.

"I offered him a drink earlier. A social faux pas?"

"Not if you find him good company."

"I find him insolent and bigoted," Ken said. "Considers himself above his helpers. Did you know that?"

"I've never discussed human or labor relations with him," Lanie said tersely. "And I'd appreciate it if you'd respect my family's privacy."

Ken drank. "He made the observation on his own, Lanie. But I get the message. Don't cultivate the hired hands."

"Master-servant etiquette isn't your problem yet, Ken."

Wincing. "But if it were, you'd prefer a policy of noblesse oblige?"

"Didn't you and Michele have servants?"

"Only one, in the town house. A Negro marvel. Michele borrowed her from the Danielles, who had a staff. What orders were necessary, Michele issued."

"You dislike ordering inferiors?"

"Subordinates, Lanie. I detest the word 'inferior.' I saw too much of it in the service, where every enlisted man is every officer's inferior."

"But you were an officer!"

"Second Lieutenant, inferior to every rank above. God, how I hated the boot-licking protocol!"

"Getting back to Beth—"

"Lanie, I called my office this morning, and there's some business I must handle personally. I'd like you to come with me. Getting away for awhile might give you a different perspective of this whole matter, and better insight."

The idea seemed to appeal to her, as a delaying tactic if nothing else. Obviously emotion had swept her farther along their course than she had expected and perhaps intended, and she needed a respite to recoup her position. "You may be right, Ken, but you go ahead alone. I have some unfinished business in Houston, and I'll fly over in a few days."

"Let me know when. I'll meet your plane."

Lanie nodded and lifted her glass. "To New Orleans."

"How romantic!" Beth chortled from the threshold. "But shouldn't you entwine arms, like in the corny old movies, and then smash glasses?"

"Bethie baby, we didn't hear you come in! What are you doing here?"

"I used to live here, Mommy girl."

"Well, I know, sweetie. But of late you've been a stranger to the realm. What brings you now?"

Beth looked questioningly at Ken. His eyes tried to reassure her about her earlier visit and confidences, and somehow she believed herself unbetrayed. "I was just riding in the woods and saw your car driving here—"

"Yes?" Lanie prompted.

She shrugged, containing her mystery. "Nothing. I—I wouldn't want to interrupt anything. I'll go now."

"Oh, you needn't hurry, dear. Come join us. Have a coke." But Beth was already fleeing like a wary animal afraid of entrapment. Lanie sighed in bewilderment. "See what I mean? You figure her out!"

"She's obviously uptight about something," Ken said. "Can't you talk about it with her?"

"I've already told you, Ken, we don't communicate very well. In foreign tongues, for all we accomplish in our few mother-daughter dialogues. She's off alone so much of the time, on that horse which I sometimes think she loves above all else on earth. Perhaps I should invite her to go to New Orleans with me? No, Mother will chaperone her adequately. And she'd probably only be moody and resentful, anyway. She went there so often with her father and me. We never missed Mardi Gras."

"Neither did Michele and I," Ken reflected somberly.

"Strange we never met at some ball or other?"

"We might have and don't remember. Most of the balls were masked, you know. People dance and sing and drink together without introduction—even make love and promptly forget it. That's the magic of Mardi Gras. But it's a seasonal spell, and the season's past. So we'll have to create our own enchantment, Lanie."

Her eyes lingered on her daughter's exit. "I hope we can, Ken, because my little witch just vanquished mine . . ."

"If a man create his own wilderness and be lost in it, he must not expect Providence to find and deliver him."

AN EVANGELIST'S HANDBOOK

CHAPTER EIGHT

The New Orleans Experiment, Mrs. Whitney
called it, and conceded that it might have some
merit, if only because it was generally enlightening
to study a species in its native habitat. At the same
time, however, she cautioned her daughter not to
attach undue importance to any appearance of
normalcy she might find, since most biological
species, man included, were able to adapt to their
environment even under adverse conditions; and
Lanie demanded irritably, "What in hell is that
supposed to mean?"

"If you don't know, I can't explain."

"Well, I'm not investigating Kenneth Steele,
Mother, nor investing anything with him except
my time."

"And your heart, remember, which is surely a
woman's most valuable and vulnerable asset."

"Then mine should be perfectly safe," Lanie
mused, "since according to my darling daughter,
my heart is an insensitive plastic object incapable
of any but synthetic emotion and mechanical response. Apparently I don't react strongly enough
to certain sentimental stimuli to suit her. I only wish
she were a little more passive. So don't worry about
me, Mother. Just keep a tight leash on my cub."

"That won't be easy without a whip and chair," Eunice declared. "But I'll do my best. Seriously, Lanine, is it possible you are going first to Houston to shop for a trousseau?"

"No, just to catch a plane," Lanie assured her.

"Well, I wouldn't bother to alert him, give him time to put his house in order. I'd take him by surprise."

"Catch him off guard? You and the FBI employ the same tactics, Mother."

"They're effective," Eunce said.

"Only with criminals, darling."

Nevertheless, Lanie arrived sans notice in mid-afternoon and took a cab from the airport to the address on the business card Ken had given her.

The aura encompassing the city was only summer haze, portending rain, but it intrigued her. Here she was, thirty-five and presumably a sophisticated woman, on her first real rendezvous. Some of her friends might find that amusing and even amasing. Her mother considered it experimental. Lanie was unaware of any particular curiosities or convictions of her own; she believed she was simply trying to discover if she loved Kenneth Steele enough to marry him.

She found a small but patently proper office in the financial district, with dark wood paneling and soft leather furniture, subdued enough to confidence in even the most timorous or skeptical investor. The secretary-receptionist, neither young nor pretty and conservatively dressed, was a prudent asset. Lanie did not think ever her mother could criticize his office atmosphere.

"Don't announce me," she cautioned, finger to lips. "It's a surprise," and opened the door marked

MR. STEELE before the bespectacled, chignoned woman could inquire or protest.

Ken glanced up from a prospectus. "Lanie! You were supposed to call, remember?"

"I thought it would be nicer this way."

He left an actively cluttered desk to embrace her. "It would be nice, anyway." Then, he said, gesturing, "Well, this is it. Not very impressive, I'm afraid. No doubt the junior officers of Hall Industries rate better layouts."

Lanie was not familiar with either the major or minor executive suites of the company. "It's adequate, Ken. Besides, I came to see you, not your office."

"Well, you're here now, and that's all that matters," he said. "My partner is out with a client, so you'll have to meet him some other time. Very dull fellow, anyway." He smiled. "Reads nothing but ticker tape and, his wife complains, quotes the market in his sleep. Where's your luggage, darling?"

"In the cab outside?"

"With the meter running? Such extravagance!" He flipped on the intercom switch, told the secretary, whom he called Mrs. Tarrant, that he was leaving for the day.

"No, appointments?" asked Lanie.

"None as important as you."

And that was the last Lanie saw of Steel & Howe, Investment Counselors. Her mother would probably have found some discreet way to question the help and examine the files, but Lanie was satisfied with what she saw: an adequate broker in an adequate establishment.

He lived in comparable adequacy: an urban complex of unimaginatively stacked bricks with windows, bright doors, and iron-banistered stairways. A stall for his sports car. A cantilevered balcony large enough for a pair of contour chairs and small metal table. No wonder the estate had awed him! Was this all seven years of marriage to a wealthy woman had netted him? No insurance, even? Had there been some kind of premarital agreement demanded by her family? It was not an uncommon practice in a misalliance.

"Don't say I didn't warn you," he said, opening the door on an apartment that could only be termed utilitarian in space and equipment. A place to survive.

"It's ample, Ken." She meant adequate but shied off the word. So much about him suddenly seemed only adequate. And Eunice was right about the visit; it was a revelation, rather like observing a specimen on a slide.

"It's a box, Lanie, but at least it's not full of bad memories. And there's no danger of getting lost, as in your labyrinth. Something cool to drink? Daiquiri? Julep?"

"Sherry, please, if you have it."

"Got it," he said. "The comfort station's down the hall—not the first door, that's a closet."

So was the bath, dimensionally. And she'd offered him a sunken marble tub and sauna!

Emerging, she saw that he'd put her bags in the bedroom, and then all she saw was the painting over the bed. A nude of a preposterously beautiful woman. Incredible breasts and hips and legs. A cascade of dark hair, oblique eyes under winged brows, voluptuous mouth. No real person could look like that! The artist had either exaggerated or painted with dazzled eyes. Lanie could imagine the emotions it would stir in any virile male. But why did he display it now? It seemed masochistic.

"That painting in the bedroom," she said, rejoining him. "The late Mrs. Steele?"

"Yes," he said.

"She was beautiful."

He nodded. "Here's your sherry. I'm sorry it's not your favorite brand."

"Fantastic figure."

"Fantastic," he agreed. "Supple, graceful, highly coordinated. Her sports activities helped, of course. In time she may have become muscular but never flabby."

"Well, if that's what it takes, I'm afraid I'm destined for flab, Lanie despaired "I hate exercise and sports bore me. Unlike my daughter, who goes in for everything from archery to spelunking."

"Her body shows it."

"You've noticed?"

"Having eyes, yes. For sixteen she's well stacked. Is that sherry drinkable? You're ignoring it like vinegar."

She swallowed the wine like medicine, clicked the glass down on the glass-topped coffeetable before the sofa and curled her legs under her, to prove she was still agile enough for such contortions.

Ken occupied an armchair opposite her. "How was your flight?"

"Commercial. Delayed, confused. Miracle of miracles, my baggage arrived with me. I prefer private planes."

"Not many people have a choice."

"Well, if you join the Club, you'll have a plane and pilot at your disposal."

She said "if" not "when." It piqued him. "Maybe I'll get a licence and fly my own, like the Late Great Man."

"You're jealous of him," she accused.

"Desperately."

"How do you think I feel, seeing *her* in there? I should think it'd be difficult to sleep with any other woman, like having three in bed."

"It's only a painting, Lanie. It has no reality. But if it offends you, I'll remove it while you're here."

"You'll remove it permanently, Ken, if we're married. You'll dispose of it completely."

"'If' again. His jaw set firmly. "No, I won't, my dear. The artist was a friend of Michele's, and it's a fine piece of work. You should recognize talent, Lanie. You know something about art."

"Sell it, then. It should bring a bundle for some lustful bachelor's pad."

"I couldn't do that, either," he said gravely. "She was my wife, and her family was prominent. They wouldn't want that painting exhibited just anywhere, and neither would I."

"Well, if you think for one goddamn moment," Lanie raged, "that I'd have it hanging in my home, forget it!"

"Why don't we both forget it for now?"

Shifting positions nervously, "I don't understand you, Ken. Why do you want a ghost like that around, haunting you day and night? Are you punishing yourself, obsessed, possessed, what? If it's possession, removing that fetish should be the first rite of exorcism."

He stood, holding his empty glass like a crystal chasm between them. "Shall we go out to dinner, cook, or have something sent in?"

"Cook," Lanie relented, ashamed of her temper. "I didn't mean to rail at you like a fishwife, Ken. I'm just tired from that wretched flight, and I have a headache for the first time in months. I hope it won't spoil our evening. Please don't think I'm a shrew about Michele."

"It's all right, Lanie. Take some aspirin and lie down. I can manage alone."

"Oh no, darling, I want to help!" She trailed him into the culinary cubicle, less than half the size of her butler's pantry. "What's on the menu?"

"Shrimp? Crab? Red snapper? We eat a lot of seafood in New Orleans. And there's a bottle of champagne on ice."

Fashioning a dishtowel apron to protect her designer dress, Lanie asked casually, "Was she a good cook?"

"Yes. She did most things well."

"But not everything?"

"Nobody's perfect, Lanie."

They put together a palatable meal and ate it in the dining alcove overlooking the courtyard. Below the windows a concrete kidney held artificially blue water. Masses of brilliant tropical blooms softened the austere brick walls and ivy disguised some of the blatant architectural errors. How could he bear living there alone, viewing that same scene from the glass inserts in his box day after day? It would give her claustrophobia!

She drank half of the champagne and put brandy in her demitasse; if she couldn't obliterate the past, at least she could blur it. And by the time they went to bed, she felt superior simply by being alive. She had purchased a contraceptive in Houston, and while she was in the bathroom, the painting of Michele was removed, and there was only the bare wall above their bare bodies.

Around midnight, with her drowsing in his arms, Ken proposed. "Let's make it legal, Lanie. We could do it here easily, in a few days. Licence, blood tests, judge. And this is a terrific place for a honeymoon."

"Oh no, darling. Not some hasty civil pudding. I want the frosted cake, even if I can't have the crown and veil. How was it with Michele?"

"Formal, and I hated it. But that's the way her family did things, and they were in complete charge. Nobody consulted me."

"Not even the bride?"

He released her. "Goddamn it, Lanie! I told you, her mother took over. The only daughter, only child. It had to be An Occasion, even if they didn't approve of the groom. And they didn't approve of me, Lanie. Why? Because Madame Danielle and Mrs. Whitney are sisters under the skin," he said bitterly. "I was nothing socially or financially. Michele's mother ruled the Mardi Gras social affairs, and mine made costumes for them. Reason enough?"

"Did your inlaws eventually soften?"

"Does stone yield with time? It grows more adamant. And if they were tolerant for Michele's sake before the accident, they were hostile afterwards. There was no understanding, compassion, forgiveness. I haven't seen them since the funeral, and that's fine with me. Monsieur Danielle is an arrogant bastard, and Madame a domineering bitch. I don't know how they produced a sweet kid like Michele, without a snobbish bone in her whole beautiful body."

Nor apparently a prudish one, Lanie thought, conscious again of the spiritual presence in the room, now the physical enchantment was over. And the creator of this haunting masterpiece? She hadn't noticed the signature, if any. Who was he, and where was he now, if not also lurking about?

"You resigned from the Danielle firm?"

"By request," Ken brooded. "The way I vacated the town house. The Ponchartrain property was Michele's, inherited from her grandmother. We put it in a joint deed, and so it's mine. But that's all I got, not even any insurance. The Danielles had been paying the premiums on her policies, and Michele neglected to change the beneficiary. She had no will, either. She didn't expect to die."

"Neither did Brian," Lannie murmured. "I guess no one ever does, actually. They might think of death, but they don't really expect it to happen."

"Tomorrow we'll go to Halcyon," Ken said. "That's the name of the summer place."

"But isn't that where—?"

"Not in the house, Lanie. The lake. I told you, don't you remember?"

"I remember, Ken—but are you trying to forget? What will I find at Halcyon? More momentos?"

"Some, naturally. People leave traces, you know, and you haven't removed all of Brian's from your life, yet, either. I saw signs at the estate. I didn't object."

"You would if you loved me."

"Lanie, is this trip some kind of test? A psychological study of Kenneth Steele, maybe, made with your mother's approval? Observe the rat in his maze, so to speak?"

Lanie squirmed. He sounded as if he'd been coached by her daughter. "Who told you that?"

"No one had to tell me, Lanie. Those historical biographies your mother helped to write read like a detective's dossiers. Christ, the 'distinguishing characteristics' she listed, including moles, warts, scars, and birthmarks! Nothing escaped her."

"Mother is thorough, all right."

99

"Fanatic," Ken said. "Ditto Madame Danielle And I had to have two such fanatics sticking pins in me."

"What about the pins you're sticking in yourself, with that replica under the bed? That's not fanatic? Hang it up again and wail incantations if you want. I won't stop you."

"Oh, hell," he muttered, pounding his pillow in fierce frustration. "It seems we can't make love without making war, Lanie. If that's the result, we can't be very good for each other, can we?"

Lanie retreated, holding the white sheet before her like a flag of truce. "I don't enjoy the battles, Ken, and I'm afraid of getting hurt."

"Hurt?"

"Love can wound, can't it? Destroy? Even kill?"

"Sure, it's a primitive instinct, so it can be violent, ruthless, savage, brutal, murderous. But nothing's going to happen to you with me, baby—not even sex unless you want it. Now please, let's try to get some sleep. Tomorrow we'll go to the country, and you just might enjoy it—if you relax and let yourself."

CHAPTER NINE

The city was fogbound, caught like a great sprawling animal in a misty web. Ships rode anchor in the harbor, only a few with perishable cargoes moved phantomlike on the river, while foghorns moaned ominously.

"I hate those sounds," Lanie said, shuddering. "Dismal, spooky. We never hear them in Woodland."

Ken was intent on driving in the ground traffic, now a frenzied tangle. "The foghorns? I grew up hearing them. They groaned during my birth, in fact, since I arrived on a foggy night. As a kid I hung around the docks, watching my father work his tail off. It was a liberal education in the unfine arts. One thing I learned early, I didn't want to follow in his footsteps. I had to do better, or die trying."

"What did you want for yourself?"

"I can tell you what I didn't want! To wrestle with tons of cotton and sugar and rice, molasses and bananas all my life and end up trying to exist on a union pension. Like most people born with a tin spoon in the mouth and brass ring in the nose, I coveted success and achievement. Horatio Alger stories were my boyhood dreams, and I admired guts and aggressiveness. Oh, I was ambitious as the devil, maybe even as ruthless and desperate." He glanced at her placid profile, which showed no signs of stress or struggle for anything. "What're you thinking, Lanie? Why then did I marry a poor little factory girl? I've already explained that. Youth and love and passion—a potent and frequently fatal combination as far as one's future is concerned. An impetuous mistake, but fortunately we both survived it. Not many young couples are so lucky. Too often they keep plodding away in a hopeless situation until it's too late'"

"Too late for what, Ken?"

"To prevent the waste and ruin of two lives'"

Morning mist turned to rain as they reached Ponchartrain and continued steadily across the twenty-four mile causeway to the north shore. The summer retreat, once part of a vast country estate, was in the Ozone Forest Belt, secluded from the beach by pines, magnolias, liveoaks, and tall japonica camellias. Stilted docks and boatstalls perched on the water. Obviously valuable property and still extensive, since the nearest neighbors were some distance away on either side. His legacy from Michele Danielle was not, then, as trivial as he had implied.

The gray-green surface of Ponchartrain was choppy now, churned by the wind that had risen with the summer storm, and deserted, the resort colony residents and visitors driven to shelter. Although a shallow lake, sixteen feet at its deepest, Ponchartrain was huge and treacherous in a squall and had claimed many drowning victims, including Mrs. Kenneth Steele.

A massive wrought-iron arch marked Halcyon, and the long driveway was paved with crushed oyster-shells. Ken parked under the porte-cochere, and they managed to get inside without getting soaked. But Lanie didn't think they'd have much use for the swimsuits they'd brought along, hers a new white bikini she wasn't anxious to wear since viewing the nude of the magnificent Michele. Still Ken seemed eager to show her the place, either to reassure her or himself about something that had not originally concerned Lanie. But on entry his mood grew noticeably somber and pensive.

"It's a marvelous hideaway, Ken. I'm surprised her people let you keep it."

"They had no choice, except to resort to court litigation to try to reclaim it. The deed was recorded in both our names. But I'm not as vindictive as they. I'd sell it back to them, for the right price. So far, however, they've made no offers. Damn this weather! It's temperamental as a woman. And it rains here almost as much as in the tropics."

Halcyon affected him, no doubt of that. He paced across the living room, restless and brooding, hands jammed in his pockets, pausing now and then to scowl at the water-wavy windows and the trees beyond writhing and groaning like giant figures in elemental frenzy. Lanie shivered, although it was not cold but damp and musty as the moss that shrouded so much of the Louisiana landscape. She could imagine everything in the closets and cupboards covered with mildew and fungi. A sepulchral odor, due to unairing, pervaded the premises, and Lanie had a vague sense of another presence. When her eyes fell on the pillow-strewn couch, she realized why: the spotted throw, imitation leopard-skin, was familiar. Michele was lying on such a coverlet in the painting. The same one?

"May I poke around, Ken?"

"Be my guest."

She indicated a closed door off the living room. "What's that?"

"Hobby room."

Lanie ventured in. Seashells, driftwood, dried flora. Easels, caked palettes, matted brushes; canvases, oils, watercolors. Tennis and badminton rackets. Golf clubs. Riding crops. Surfboards. Water skis.

"Michelle dabbled," he explained. "And collected things."

Michele was restless, Lanie thought. Was Michele also lonely and unhappy? Fickle, temperamental, capricious? Unable to pursue anything for long? Incomplete arrangements, collages, decoupages, projects. Partially painted pictures of stormy seas, agitated trees, birds in flight. Not very neat, either, if this was the mess she'd left. Was her personal life as disorderly, her emotions as rampant and unsettled? Dabbler, collector, sports enthusiast. How else had Michele occupied and amused herself? The "sweet kid" image did not quite tally with this chaotic scene. Why didn't Ken clean and straighten it up, dispose of the fragments and remnants? For the same reason he cherished the painting and photographs, because they were all sacred memorabilia and fetishes to him? And did he return periodically to practice his peculiar idolatry?

"Are those the skis?" she asked.

He nodded gravely. "And that's the towline in the corner. You can see where it snapped. It was all examined by the law, Lanie. Since I was the only witness, there was an inquest. I have a copy of the findings, if you're interested. The verdict was accidental death by drowning, probably due to her being rendered unconscious by a ski injury to the head."

"I wasn't questioning the verdict, Ken. Why are you so defensive about it?"

His shrug was more of a shudder. "Maybe because I feel guilty. I should have inspected that rope before towing her on it. The weak point might have been apparent. Perhaps it'd been caught in a motor blade, some fibers destroyed. That's what the authorities surmised, anyway, assuming it had somehow brushed our own propeller on a turn or slalom, or while slack during a spill. She'd been skiing less than a half-hour when it happened, so the tow had to be defective. Her parents will never forgive me; they actually hold me responsible for her death, figuring I was negligent, and I suppose I can't honestly blame them. It's hard to take the loss of an only child. Michele was all they had, and they worshiped her."

"That's only natural," Lanie said, thinking of her own daughter. She would hate anyone she thought had hurt or destroyed Beth. "How old was Michele?"

"Twenty-four when we married, thirty-one when —" He picked up a conch shell, fondled the smooth pink interior, replaced it on the cluttered table and picked up some dry seaweed, crumbling it absently. Then his fingers traced a twisted piece of driftwood. He was punishing himself in there, Lanie realized; trying and convicting himself, and she reprieved him by moving out.

Rain splashed harder now, coming in torrents, and the wind raged in the trees. The lake had become an angry, horizonless cauldron of boiling whitecaps. Some men were sexually aroused by elemental fury, and Lanie rather hoped that Ken would be similarly stimulated. But he was pre-occupied, as he'd been since their arrival. Oh, this house was bad for him and for their relationship! Yet, he was obviously drawn to it, the magnetism evidently stronger than any repugnance he may have felt.

"Do you have that diary, Ken?"

"What diary?"

"The one you mentioned to my mother."

"No, I don't, Lanie. Not here, anyway. My aunt has it. It really belongs to her, my father's sister, since it was found in her possessions."

Why had he seemed surprised by her question and hesitated before replying? Was there some other diary on his mind, one belonging to Michele perhaps?

"Have you given up that search, Ken?"

"Almost," he said. "My aunt gave me some sound advice, I think: Let sleeping dogs lie."

"Dogs?"

"She meant, don't disturb the dead."

"Lest you disturb the living?"

"That's the moral, I believe. Aunt Selma's a wise old bird. Maybe I should listen to her. Some things we're better off not knowing, Lanie. I don't care that much any more, actually. It seemed important at the time, less so now."

Served its purpose, her mother would say; achieved the entry he wanted. Progress would depend on his own personality and ingenuity. More and more she was thinking like Eunice, and it disturbed Lanie. She didn't want to speculate or prejudge that way. It was emotionally abrasive and detrimental and could wreck their rapport.

She settled in the living room, a big square salon with glass expanses facing the lake, decorated in sunny yellows and jungle greens. Ken stood against the fireplace mantel, the uncleaned hearth gray with last winter's ashes.

"That artist who painted Michele, Ken—what's his name?"

"Chandre. Paul Chandre."

"Does he live in New Orleans?"

"Yes. He has a studio in the Quarter. Why? Want your portrait painted?"

"Just curious. He's good, no denying that. Is he also famous?"

On the mantelshelf were brass candlesticks with half-burned candles, a jade Buddha with a bellyful of Oriental incense, and more rare shells and sea objects. Ken touched a piece of coral before answering. "There're many good artists, Lanie. Precious few ever achieve recognition, much less fame and wealth. Chandre makes a living but not much more. He used to do charcoal sketches at one of the better nightclubs. He's quick, can catch a subject in minutes, and the likeness is remarkable. During Mardi Gras he does hundreds of tourists for ten to fifty bucks apiece, or whatever the traffic will bear, and largely coasts on the proceeds till the next season. Not very ambitious, Mr. Chandre, and rather lazy."

Lanie wondered if his late wife had been Chandre's sponsor, benefactress, angel—a connoisseur and patron of the arts or only a dilettante. "Is his portrayal of Michele honest?"

"How do you mean, honest?"

"Accurate. Was she really that beautiful?"

"I thought so. So did Chandre, apparently."

"I feel pallid and like Milquetoast by comparison," Lanie said, wistfully. "She gives me an inferiority complex, in fact. All that dark voluptuous beauty. Sensual, sultry, exotic, The leopard prop was apropos, all right." Indicating the spotted cloth on which she lounged, "Is that it?"

"Yes, Michele loaned it to Chandre for the sitting."

"Here?"

"No, his studio. The light was better there."

"And you didn't mind her posing that way?"

Ken lit a cigarette before replying. "I didn't know anything about it. Michele gave me the painting as a birthday gift."

Lanie couldn't resist quipping, "At a surprise party?"

That angered him, and he severed the subject abruptly. "Enough about Michele! It doesn't look as if this monsoon is going to end soon. Shall we go back to the city?"

"We just got here," Lanie protested. "Besides, that causeway is creepy in a storm."

"Well, don't worry about the house. It's built like a fortress, concrete piers deep in the ground. Even hurricanes can't phase it much—maybe ripping off shutters, shingles, and gallery but no more. Michele and I sat out both Carla and Camille here without a scratch. Are you getting hungry? There's some staples in the pantry and fridge. We can snack. How about some wine, cheese, and crackers?"

"Later," Lanie said, and it occurred to her that she hadn't yet enjoyed any of the cuisine for which New Orleans was famous. Tomorrow perhaps, after her visit to the Vieux Carré ... for she intended to call on Paul Chandre, alone. She would invent some pretext, shopping or hairdresser. Ken might not be fooled, but it didn't matter. She had to meet Chandre, and her ruse could be a request for a charcoal sketch.

Lightening struck a power line in the vicinity, casting the room into sudden darkness, and Ken began lighting candles. "Hell of a day I picked to go to the country! These tempests rarely last this long, however, and often vanish as rapidly as they appear—unless there's real trouble brewing in the Gulf. You're not afraid, are you?"

"No," Lanie murmured. But she was nervously tense and apprehensive and wished he would find a better way than talk to distract her.

He tossed his cigarette into the dead ashes, and promptly lit another with candleflame. "Hey, I think it's slacking off a bit. Good thing we stayed. Let's have a drink, shall we? I think you're nervous as a witch . . ."

The storm died swiftly, blowing out to sea, thunder rumbling like distant cannonade off the coastal ramparts. The lights flicked on. Ken extinguished the candles. Soon the sun was out, sparkling on the calmed water, and the air was heavy with the fragrance of wet camellias, jasmine, tuberoses, oleanders. They walked down to the beach and along the shore, barefoot.

"Did you entertain much here, Ken? It seems like an ideal place for parties."

"We had some, but not many or large. Michele liked intimate, informal affairs. She was not social- ite Madame Danielle is, thank God. I couldn't have stood that kind of pressure. Our guests were sort of avant-garde."

"Ours weren't, unless you consider ranchers and riders, hunters and fox hunters avant-garde."

"Well, I've met some pretty bizarre characters in the Horsey Set. I remember being invited to ride in a hunt at an old plantation on the River Road. My God, some of them looked and acted like antebellum spooks! And they were attended by Negroes they treated like slaves."

"Let's not get political, darling. I get enough of that static from my daughter. The little rebel. I hope Mother is managing to cope with her. I miss her, but she seemed eager for me to leave. One less disciplinarian, I guess. Gee, the sun is getting hot! I'd better find some shade before I look like a redskin."

"You don't like that color?"

"Red?"

"Indian."

"Well, I certainly wouldn't want to be one. I wouldn't want to be yellow or brown or black, either. Would you?"

"I guess not," Ken said. "Want to swim after sundown? I think there's an early moon. We won't need suits· Michele and I never used them at night·"

"Did she also ski nude?"

"Only if there was no one in sight. She sunbathed raw, too. Liked to be tan all over. What's wrong with that?"

"Nothing, if nudity is your bag."

"Why don't you say it, Lanie? You think Michele was not only immodest but perhaps wanton?"

They seemed always on the narrow edge of hostility and breach over this creature. "Those are your words, Ken, and I don't care to pursue them. I could do with some of that wine and cheese now..."

Somehow, in the moonlight, Halcyon seemed awesome, even menacing. Isolated in trees and shrubbery, only the tall chimneys limned the night sky. The bulky boatsheds and the water slapping somberly against the wharf and jetty poles. Lanie couldn't enjoy the Ovidian frolic in the surf, and she didn't think that Ken did much, either. He scarcely looked at her body, and then with little lust or admiration. She waited in vain for intimate overtures. He glanced intermittently at the shed which no doubt contained the craft involved in the tragedy, as if compelled to torture himself.

Returning to the house, towel-draped and uncommunicative, Lanie capriciously determined to seduce him on the couch and the leopard throw. If the damn thing was sacred to him, then she would force him to profane it. But she had to work at it, for he was maddeningly passive. When at last she imagined herself about to succeed one way or another, he pushed her away and down on the floor.

"Goddamn it, Lanie!"

She was startled, stunned. "You don't like that?"

"Not as a ploy. That's how she used it, to get her way, and I was wax in her velvet claws."

"Who?"

"Michele! Who else have we been examining all day? Let's dissect your husband and marriage for a change. Did you practice fellatio-cunnilingus regularly, as a routine procedure, or only when you wanted something bad enough to make the effort? Tell me!"

"Damned if I will! And just what do you think I want bad enough to coax you that way?"

"You want me to denounce Michele, that's what! To say you're better looking and better built and better in bed. To say she was a bitch, that I never loved her and am glad she's gone. Maybe even that I killed her!"

"Did you?"

Instantly he struck her, hard across the face, cutting her mouth inside. She felt the membrane split against her teeth, tasted blood on her tongue.

"You bastard," she murmured. "Sadistic brute."

"Lanie." He was on his knees before her, humble, penitent. "Oh, God, I'm sorry. I lost my temper. But why did you say that? Do you think I did kill her?"

"Let me alone, Ken." Enough rationality had returned to mortify her. "Please, just let me alone."

"Did I hurt you, baby? Let me see."

"I'm all right," she insisted, swallowing the salty-sweet seepage in her mouth. "Just don't touch me now, Ken."

"I warned you I could be violent, remember? Why do you keep challenging and provoking me? And why can't you believe what I tell you about the accident?"

"Do you think I'd be here now if I didn't? That I'd come to a place like this with a suspected murderer! But no man has ever hit me before, Ken, and if ever you do again—"

"Dearest, I won't, I promise you. Forgive me, please, and come upstairs with me now. Let me make love to you. We'll do it all, everything—but for the right reasons, Lanie. It's ersatz otherwise, and capitulation, and I don't want any part of it. That's what I resented—your motives, not method. Do you understand?"

She was crying, trembling. "I don't know."

"Lanie, there's so little in life that's worthwhile. And so much sham and hypocrisy. If it has to be applied to sex as well, then nothing is real or true or natural . . ."

"What about her velvet claws, Ken?"

"I shouldn't have said that."

"But you did. Was she a cat in heat?"

"Come along, darling."

"No, Ken."

"Yes," he said. "We have to make this up, Lanie, if it takes all night."

He urged her to her feet, supporting, guiding her toward the stairway. Together they climbed, slowly, like naked figures ascending in a dream or fantasy. Lanie didn't know if the room they eventually entered was his, hers, or theirs, and after awhile it didn't matter. Love was its own enchantment, its own obliteration.

CHAPTER TEN

Except for the sore spot inside her cheek, tender to the touch of tongue and teeth, the incident was, if not entirely forgotten, tacitly ignored. But the return trip was on the silent side, and Lanie didn't have to devise excuses to be alone the next morning. Ken said he had some VIP appointments, fixed his own breakfast while she feigned sleep, put on his business clothes and kissed her awake.

Lanie affected a yawn and languid stretch. "Morning love. Leaving already? Why didn't you wake me earlier? I can cook bacon and eggs."

"Thought you needed the rest," he said. "There's some coffee in the perk. I have to go to the salt mines, make my daily bread. You don't mind?"

"Of course not. I'll browse in the shops."

"Well, take care if you go to the Quarter. Stay with the crowds and off the side streets. Parts of it are rough, you know, and getting rougher every day. I'll see you this evening. We'll go out on the town if you like. There's an extra key on the dresser." His parting kiss was so light and swift, Lanie scarcely felt it.

She showered and, between sips of strong black coffee heavily laced with chicory, put on a yellow linen sundress and sandals and brushed her bright

114

hair into a smooth side part. The telephone directory listed a Paul Chandre, on Royal Street. She dialed the number, counted ten rings, and was about to hang up when a drowsy male voice answered.

"Mr. Chandre? Paul Chandre, the artist?"

"Artist," he corrected, "not *the*. There's more than one here, unfortunately."

"I'm Mrs. Lanine Hall, Mr. Chandre. I've heard about your marvelous charcoal portraits and would like one."

"Jesus, lady, what time is it?"

"Ten o'clock. Nine-fifty, to be exact."

"I got to bed at dawn," he yawned.

"Oh, I'm so sorry I disturbed you. But I'm in town for the day only, and I admire your work. Could you possibly accommodate me? The fee is immaterial."

"Give me an hour or so to get organized, ma'am."

"Certainly. Eleven okay?"

He agreed and hung up.

Lanie ordered a taxi, wondering how she would broach the subject to Paul Chandre. Casual reference, or direct approach? Presumably he was not a moron and would see through whatever strategy she employed.

Tourists swarmed over the French Quarter. The day people, hoppers, a different species from the night crawlers. These were groupers, families with kids and cameras, and senior citizens on packaged tours.

Lanie's previous contact with the Vieux Carré had been essentially physical—food, drink, music, merry-making. She had dined in its restaurants and watched the entertainment in its clubs; browsed in its art galleries and antique shops. She had en-

joyed the unusual atmosphere—the translucent
light at dawn which seemed diffused through an
opalescent screen, the pearly river mists that frequently hovered in autumn and winter, the weight
of centuries that permeated the very bricks and
stones. But she had never known or met anyone
who actually lived in this Montmartre on the right
bank of the Mississippi, a community as unique
and remote from the rest of the city as Greenwich
Village from Manhattan, Soho from London, and
the Left Bank from Paris.

Even the architecture possessed its own charisma.
Some of the ancient houses had been beautifully
restored, others seemed about to crumble into the
narrow streets and sequestered courtyards, as at
the address to which the cab delivered Lanine Hall.
Dampness, the leprosy of paint and plaster, had
defaced the flesh-colored stucco walls, and the
multi-patched sidewalk was a comic mosaic of
amateurish effort. The wood stoop was rotting
away. The overhead gallery sagged precariously,
its lacy iron banister as rusty as the knocker on the
door.

Paul Chandre's "organization" had consisted primarily of putting on a pair of low-hipped striped
pants and a paint-spattered shirt open to the navel,
not for effect but lack of buttons. Lanie did not
consider him handsome; his sandy hair was too long
and shaggy, his skin too sallow, his tall angular body
too lean and dissipated. She could not imagine
him engaging in any of Michele's strenuous outdoor
activities. Still he was not unattractive, and far
from repulsive; and no doubt he lived a Bohemian
life that could be interesting and exciting. He was
drinking bittersweet café au laît in the living area
of his studio and offered his visitor a cup. She

accepted to busy her hands, which suddenly seemed awkward and clammy in her white gloves.

"So you're a fan of mine?" he began tentatively. "Since I'm practically anonymous in the art circles and have never exhibited in a renowned gallery—may I ask where and how you heard of me, Mrs. Hall?"

"From a friend."

"Friend?" he insisted.

"Kenneth Steele."

His indigo eyes widened perceptibly, then narrowed again to focus steadily on her face, as if to gain perspective. "In that case, I think I know the work you mean."

"Well, I'm no art critic, Mr. Chandre, but I'd call it a masterpiece. Inspired."

"The subject was an inspiration."

"You knew her well?"

"From birth. She was my niece."

Lanie almost gasped, "Your *niece?*"

"That's right. Her mother, Luise, is my sister. Steele didn't tell you that?"

"Probably, I just forgot." But he hadn't told her, she was positive. Ken had distinctly said that the painter was a friend of his wife, not her uncle. Why should he deliberately conceal their kinship?

"Luise is considerably older than I," Chandre continued his assault on her senses. "I came along late in our mother's life, at the climacteric. I was five when Luise married Peter Danielle, so you can see I was a very young uncle to her child. We used to play together."

"How nice," Lanie murmured inanely.

"Only when we were children. Later on, it got difficult. Tedious. But you came for a sketch, didn't you? However, charcoal is the wrong medium for

117

you, Mrs. Hall. Your coloring is perfect for pastel, and I do it very well."

"What?"

"The portrait, ma'am." Smiling guilelessly, "That is why you came, isn't it?"

"Not really," Lanie confessed.

"I didn't think so. And I believe I'm entitled to an explanation. Are you and Kenneth Steele more than friends? Considering marriage possibly?"

"Possibly."

"How did you meet?"

"It's a long story."

"But you're not from New Orleans? That's a Texas accent, if my ear serves."

"A little place called Woodland."

"Never heard of it."

"Not many people have."

"Your name is not so anonymous, however. Are you by any chance one of the East Texas Halls?"

"Brian Tyson Hall's widow," Lanie replied.

Chandre whistled softly. "The lucky bastard. Ken, not your late husband." Discarding his coffee cup he stepped to an antique etagere and removed a small, exquisite cloisonné box from a cache in the books. Lanie imagined it contained precious gems until he opened the lid and offered to share its contents with her. "You use this stuff?"

"Marijuana? No, thank you, I don't."

"Mind if I do?"

What could she say? "Not at all."

Chandre lighted the joint and inhaled deeply, closing his eyes briefly, luxuriating in whatever sensation the weed provided. "What do you want to know about my niece?"

"Everything, but I don't know where to begin."

The smoke had the odor of strong tea; wisps of

it floated about the room like blown feathers. "Just ask," he invited with a languid gesture. "I'm not shy or secretive."

"Well, were they happy together, Ken and Michele?"

"That depends on your conception of happiness. If you mean were they in love, the answer is no. Not Michele, anyway. She was in love with me, and me with her. We couldn't marry because of blood relationship. Against the marital laws, you know, that degree of consanguinity. Incest. Biblical, eugenics laid down in Leviticus and still upheld in our society. Shocked, Mrs. Hall?"

"Not particularly," Lanie lied. "But did Ken know?"

"About our blood or our emotional relationship?"

"Both."

"He knew we were related," Chandre said. "And unless he was a naïve and absolute fool, which he's not, he knew the rest of it, too. We don't like each other, never have, but that's only the natural antipathy of two men in love with the same woman. Actually, he was pretty much of a gentleman about it. Good sport, to give the devil his due. Maybe he considered half a love better than none. And so he still has that painting? Why does he torture himself that way!" He paused, pondering the ember of his cigarette. "But I shouldn't criticize him. I have a whole gallery of Micheles. Come along, if you're interested. I'll show you."

He led her to his studio, at the rear of the building. Through the grimy windows and skylight, Lanie could see the courtyard rank with bougainvillea, wisteria, clematis, honeysuckle. A naked female statue stood in a stagnant fountain holding a broken vessel, and several sparrows splashed in a

119

lichen-covered birdbath. Weeds—perhaps marijuana—flourished in the neglected garden.

Chandre released the cord of a pall-like drapery
secluding one end of the studio. "Voilà!"

Lanie viewed an incredible collection represent-
ing the child, the girl, the woman, the flesh and the
spirit. Every conceivable pose and expression, every
stage of dress and undress, from an adorable little
Renoir-type moppet in ruffled pink pinafore and
beribboned bonnet, to a Botticelli goddess in white
chiffon, to a Titian vixen on stark black velvet. And
several nebulous faces and tenuous figures in mists
and clouds, so ethereal and illusory, they could only
have been inspired by haunting dreams and vague
visions, yet ironically emerged as his true artistic
triumphs.

"You don't forget a woman like that," he said
reverently. "A face, a body like that. Don't expect
Steele to forget, and if you marry him, be prepared
to live with a ghost."

Lanie was speechless.

Chandre dragged deeply on the sustaining smoke.
"Michele always believed she'd return after death.
Her spirit never really left me. I feel her presence
here often, and I know she's as restless and unhappy
in her other life as she was in this one. That's why
I keep painting her. It's also why I use pot and acid
and speed occasionally. I don't know what opiate
Ken uses. Probably booze, but I can't muster much
sympathy for the poor bastard."

Having inhaled the last possible puff from the
marijuana cigarette, he destroyed it, saving a few
particles, which he placed like a savory eucharist on
his tongue. "You're staring, Mrs. Hall. Do I sound
mad? I think I am, slightly, and I hope so. Because
it's an insane world, and insanity helps to make it

endurable. Her death was such a tragic waste. It made no sense, no sense at all."

"You mean the accident?"

Nodding morosely, "It shouldn't have happened. Michele was an excellent skier and swimmer. A rope breaks, and she drowns. Killed by her own skis, essentially. One of those freaky, crazy things that nobody can explain. All I know, she's gone—and living without her is hell."

"But you don't blame Ken?"

"I did, at first, for his negligence. But maybe he couldn't help it. Maybe he was too confused to know what to do until it was too late. And maybe he was simply too tired to think clearly. Michele was hard to keep up with. Hyperactive, frustrated, she drove herself at a reckless, frenzied pace. She'd spend hours at tennis and badminton, ride a horse until it dropped, swim and ski as if she were possessed." His face slacked in brooding reflection. "I'd get exhausted just watching her play. Ken couldn't take it, either, although he tried. But Michele, poor darling, was insatiable in everything, including sex. I don't imagine Steele was much deprived because of me, or vice versa."

The sweet kid, Lanie thought. Oh, the darling little sex kitten with the velvet claws! So Ken had lied about her character, too! Did he actually condone her lust and perfidy? If so, then among those paintings should be at least one of the willing cuckold with traditional phallus-horns. It made his fanatic defense of Michele and physical abuse of herself at Halcyon contemptible.

"Do you live in the Quarter for art's sake, Mr. Chandre?"

"Not entirely. I'm broke. Blew my inheritance long ago. The family black sheep and prodigal son. I get by, though, and I don't give a damn any more. I was never as ambitious as Steele." He waited but Lanine remained silent. "What about the portrait, Mrs. Hall?"

"Some other time," Lanie demurred. "I'm afraid I'm not up to posing now." Her eyes swept the gallery jealousy, longing to destroy it, rip the canvases to shreds and splash gory pigment over the remains. "Besides, after La Belle Michele, how could anyone else offer much inspiration?"

"Don't underestimate yourself," he said, and his professional observation made her feel visually disrobed "You have excellent features and bone structure I'd like very much to paint you *Au naturel*, naturally."

She was ironically amused. "I may let you, if I marry Mr. Steele—as a surprise birthday present."

He smiled appreciatively, leaning against a table cluttered with art supplies, and crossing his thin arms on his hollow chest. "*Are* you going to marry him?"

"I haven't decided yet."

"You have nothing to gain, you know. Neither did Michele, since there were many others she could have chosen. God, what an incongruous match that was! The Danielles acted like mourners at the wedding. I was best man and felt like a pallbearer."

"Why did it take place, then?"

"Michele thought marriage might camouflage our affair, which plagued the family, and that she could control Steele, since he was nuts about her and she represented a lot of things he coveted in life. But it was a mistake all the way around. Nothing could separate Michele and me, except death, and we even considered a suicide pact.

Might have carried it out too, if fate hadn't intervened."

"Poor Ken," Lanie murmured.

"Yeah, the bourgeois boy who married an heiress. And he must have known she didn't love him. What did he expect? To live happily ever after?"

"Do you know his family?"

"I met them only once, at the wedding. His father's dead now. His mother's in a home somewhere, sick. I think there's an old maiden aunt still living. They were pathetic and miserable in the reception line. I felt sorry for them."

"Poor Ken," Lanie repeated like a sorrowful litany.

"Oh, he had his consolations. Plenty of money. Prestige position with the family firm. And a few babes. I guess he was entitled, under the circumstances. But he also cheated on his first wife. Dorene divorced him for chasing. So don't get the idea that he was a long-suffering martyr, or that Michele's death destroyed him. He was prostrate at her funeral, but he recovered."

"Where is she buried?" Lanie asked quietly.

"Cypress Grove Cemetery. The family tomb."

"Thank you for seeing me, Mr. Chandre."

"Paul," he suggested, "and I tried to cooperate. Did Ken know you planned to visit me?"

"I'm sure he suspects."

"Good luck," he said, showing her out. "I'll keep that painting offer open."

CHAPTER ELEVEN

Lanie was afraid she would faint before she could flee the leprous pink house. Her head ached fiercely, her heart was a trip-hammer in her breast, she felt weak and nauseous. No taxi in sight, but a hansom had just deposited its occupants, two elderly ladies in summery florals, at an antique shop, and Lanie promptly hired it.

The Negro driver, an anachronism in his vehicle and livery, inquired politely, "Where to, ma'am?"

"Just drive around the Quarter."

The hatted horse could have followed the familiar route blindfolded, and the informative monologue from the box was lost on the preoccupied passenger. At Jackson Square, Lanie dismissed the carriage and strolled trancelike along the sidewalk galleries, where more than art was exhibited and peddled in the spire-shadows of St. Louis Cathedral. What was their religion, Michele's and Chandre's? Hedonism? Had they indulged in drugs together, held orgies inspired by his pornographic paintings of her?

Somehow she found herself in a taxi heading for Cypress Grove Cemetery, inquiring at the office for the location of the Danielle mausoleum. She read the registry containing Michele Danielle Steele's vital statistics, as if to convince herself that the birth, death and entombment had actually occurred, and then looked for the site amid the magnolias and oaks draped in moss mourning veils. As she had expected, it was an elaborate stone structure embellished with sculpture, as befitted aristocracy. Generations of the family had undoubtedly been interred there, via the custom of burning the wood coffins after a suitable passage of time and placing the bones in a crypt. The heavy engraved bronze door was locked, and Lanie assumed that Ken possessed a key, unless the irate and vindictive clan had forced him to surrender it. Did he visit her hallowed niche, bring flowers, meditate, brood, worship? "You don't forget a woman like that," Chandre had said. "A face, a body like that. Don't expect Steele to forget—and if you marry him, be prepared to live with a ghost."

Lanie was not prepared for such company. She returned to the apartment, made a plane reservation for Houston, and was packing when Ken came in.

"What're you doing, Lanie?"

"Going home."

He didn't seem much surprised. "You saw Paul Chandre?"

"I saw him," Lanie admitted.

"And?"

Snapping a bag shut, she faced him, demanding, "Why have you been lying to me, Ken? Practically everything you told me about Michele and your marriage was a lie!"

He tossed his briefcase into a chair, angry and embarrassed. "What did you expect me to do, Lanie? Berate, condemn her? She was my wife for seven years!"

"And Paul Chandre's mistress a lot longer! His eternal love, his idol, and his *niece*. Not her friend, Ken, but her uncle, her mother's brother! Surely you knew that?"

"Some of it, not all—not in the beginning, anyway."

"He has a shrine to her memory, Ken. A private gallery to knock your eyes out. He was painting her raw in every attitude while she was still a child. How could her parents have condoned such corruption? If any male relative of mine—or any man whatever—dared commit such a moral atrocity with my daughter, I'd have him in a cage, or murder him in cold blood! Their affair was incest of a high degree, Ken. And still you loved her, adored her, considered her an angel—your precious, perfidious, lascivious Michele! You expect me to believe that?"

Moving to the bar, he said, "I'm not sure I care what you believe any more, Lanie. I'm tired of your suspicions and distrust. Your innuendos and accusations. You went on the sly to Chandre, like a detective hunting evidence of a crime. You're pretty clandestine yourself, lady."

"Only because you exploded like a madman last night and struck me in defense of her! I figured immediately I saw that nude in your bedroom that Michele the Magnifique was more sinner than saint, and you were trying to sanctify logical reason for such posthumous beatification."

His head was bent over a decanter; he did not look up from the absinthe he was pouring. "To conceal a motive for murdering her?"

"Yes!" Lanie screamed the word.

"You're hysterical," he said quietly.

126

"Oh, Ken, I can't stand this farce and deception any longer! Lies, half-truths, fanatic veneration. Michele was a tramp, a bitch, a whore, and you know it. You couldn't have loved her as much as you pretend, and the marriage couldn't have been happy. Furthermore, Chandre said you cheated on her, too. And that Dorene divorced you for infidelity."

"Did he also tell you that Dorene was screwing around? That half of Fort Dix laid her? I let her charge me, and you can call that more of my misguided chivalry. But that wasn't the case with Michele, until I discovered that Paul Chandre was more than a devoted uncle to her. The sonofabitch! Spilling his guts—and to a stranger, yet. Was he freaked out on pot or something?"

"He loved her, Ken. Her death destroyed him. He imagines her spirit comforts him. He tries to paint her soul, and it's his best work. Oh, yes, he loved her!"

"So did I, Lanie. Regardless of what she was, I loved her. I consoled myself with others while she shacked up with Chandre, but it was diversion and escape, nothing more. I couldn't get serious, and I damned sure didn't consider loving again until you came along. Our meeting seemed predestined."

"Oh, really!" she scoffed. "Wasn't it all planned, Ken? Didn't you determine to meet Brian Hall's widow, one way or another? I bet you have a portfolio of clippings about us, and a prospectus on me! The ambitious Mr. Steele, and his aspirations toward the higher altitudes—the social and financial stratosphere! Didn't Michele Chandre Danielle represent those goals to you? Wouldn't you have married her in spite of everything?"

"No, goddamn it, I wouldn't have! And if you

believe I'm that kind of greedy, grubbing, mercenary bastard—"

"Convince me otherwise," Lanie challenged. "Produce that mythical diary. Prove to me that Matthew and Sybil Steele actually existed, in Woodland County, or anywhere else?"

His glass slapped the bar. "Come on!"

"Where?"

"You want proof? I'll give it to you."

"No, you've got a wild look. I'm not going anywhere with you, now or ever again. Oh, God, I wish I'd never seen you, Kenneth Steele! I wish I'd never come here, and I'm going back to Texas as soon as possible."

"Lanie," he pleaded wearily, as a man over a routine labor, "I can't convince you if you won't let me. I only want to take you to my aunt. Must I kidnap you? I could, you know, and hold you for a fat ranson, if I were desperate as you've implied. Come with me, please. It won't take long."

"Ken, if you're lying to me again," she threatened, "I swear I'll kill you!"

"I'll help you," he said.

Selma Steele was a mite of a woman, five feet in a hard stretch, prune-wrinkled and sloe-eyed. She lived alone in the Irish Channel section, where many longshoremen formerly made their homes, and she was rocking on the porch of the old shotgun house which she had purchased to be near her late brother and his family.

Ken had grown up in the neighborhood, playing on its dirty streets, watched drunken sailors and stevedores stagger in and out of the saloons and brawl in the gutters, and prostitutes solicit on the banquettes. His little sister had died in the slum; he'd attended the dreary schools, and despised it.

Ironically, not far away, was the aristocratic Garden District, to which the Channel urchins sometimes boldly ventured to gape at the imposing mansions and enchanting gardens. The old Danielle homestead was there, nostalgically preserved in addition to other residences in both the city and country. All the youngsters had coveted the ante-bellum castles. But none, least of all Big Joe Steele's kid, had imagined he would ever enter, much less live in one.

Ken introduced Lanie. "Aunt Selma, this is Mrs. Hall, the lady I told you about. She would like to see that old journal of yours."

A seventy-year-old face does not register emotion easily, but Lanie detected reluctance and evasion on Selma Steele's. "Now, Kennie, you know what I told you about that. Why don't you just forget it? What difference can it make now? Let your ancestors rest in peace, wherever they are. You just make mystery and problems for yourself, son."

"Where's the diary, Auntie?"

"Where it's always been and belongs—my trunk in the attic. And I'm not climbing after it now, my old legs can't bear the strain." Her dark eyes appraised Lanie. "Believe me, Mrs. Hall, it's not worth the effort. Some pages missing, some hardly legible, others in French."

"Lanie?" Ken beckoned, opening the screen door.

"It's not necessary, Ken."

"You thought so an hour ago."

"Don't bother, Ken."

Feminine caprice always exasperated him. "Are you sure? We're here now, and it's no trouble."

"It's all right, really." She smiled at the old lady,

who was peering at her like an ancient owl. "I—I just wanted to meet some of Ken's family."

"Not many of us left," she said sadly. "So terrible about his poor mother."

Ken interrupted, "I haven't told her about Mom yet."

"Of course you have," Lanie lied. "Don't you remember? You said she was in a nursing home, ill."

Selma gave a mournful sigh. "You must go and see her more, Kennie, even if she doesn't know you."

"I go as often as I can, Auntie." He bent and kissed her corrugated cheek, and she sent up a stringy hand to touch him lovingly. "I'll call you tomorrow, dear."

"Must you hurry away?"

"Mrs. Hall is anxious to get back to Texas. She's leaving this evening."

"Oh? I'm sorry. I'd like to know her better."

"Thank you," Lanie said, taking her hand. "I'm sure we'll meet again, Miss Steele. Goodbye."

"Goodbye, my dear. And please, be kind to my nephew, he's all I have in the world."

Driving away, Ken said, "I didn't tell you about my mother, Lanie, but Chandre did, didn't he?"

"He said she was in a home somewhere."

"She had a stroke. Her mind is gone. The doctors hold no hope for her recovery."

"When did it happen?"

"Soon after Michele's accident. She insisted on attending the inquest. It was a severe shock and too much for her. She was afraid the Danielles would try to punish me somehow, more than they did."

"But you told me your mother was a seamstress in a costume shop," Lanie recalled.

"She was, before the stroke. And it was stupid of me to lie about it, but I didn't know then we'd become involved with each other. It seemed pointless to go into detail about family troubles and woes."

"Maybe she's just senile, Ken?"

"No, senility is a complication, all right. But she suffered permanent brain damage and will simply vegetate the rest of her life. She's insane, but it's not hereditary, you know. That's not why Michele and I didn't have children. I'm afraid I lied about that, too. Michele took precautions. She dared not risk impregnation by her uncle, because there *are* some half-wit genes in that inbred clan. Their's wasn't the first or only case of incest, merely the most recent. A hundred years ago the Chandres all married relatives of one degree or another. Seemed to have a penchant, or curse, for falling in love with each other. And themselves. Michele was a narcissist to boot. She probably worshiped with her lover at her own shrine."

Lanie was silent, and he continued doggedly, "Are you satisfied about the diary, that it does exist?"

"Yes, and I'm sorry I got hysterical, Ken."

"What happens now, Lanie?"

"I'll cancel my plane reservation."

"Beyond that?"

Lanie shrugged. "I don't know, Ken. I want to think about it. It's been one revelation after another, adding up to total confusion. I'm exhausted, mentally and physically. I'll have to recuperate more than my perspective, and I'll need time."

"How much time, Lanie? A few weeks? Months? Years, maybe? Forever? How long am I supposed to wait?"

"That's up to you, isn't it?"

His face was saturnine in the gathering dusk, profiled in shadow. "I guess it is," he said softly. "Yes, I guess it is, Lanie."

CHAPTER TWELVE

"Hi, Mom!" Beth greeted her mother on her return. "You look beat."

"It's a long trip by car," Lanie said.

"Why didn't you fly, or order a company sky chariot?"

"Ken wanted to bring his own transportation."

"Can't blame him for that. It's a drag without wheels. Grandma wouldn't let me use hers while you were gone, and I couldn't find your keys. If it weren't for my trusty steed—"

Ken was bringing in the luggage, and Lanie said edgily, "Listen, you two! That's not the Invisible Man out there, so stop pretending you don't see him. He's real, he exists, and you can't just ignore him."

Beth asked sullenly, "Did you get married in New Orleans?"

Lanie touched her cheek tenderly. "No, darling, I did not. I wouldn't do that without your knowledge."

"Then why did he come back with you?"

"I invited him," Lanie said. "We have to resolve some issues between us, and we couldn't do it from a distance. He'll be staying at the estate again. We have an agreement."

133

"Don't you mean arrangement?" Mrs. Whitney suggested.

Ken entered the hall as Beth was departing, yelling over her shoulder, "Don't wait chow on me! I'll grab a pizza or something. Off for a ride now."

Eunice sighed. "What a time I had keeping track of that gypsy! She disappears, Lanie, for hours on end, heaven only knows where. If you don't take a firmer hand with her, and soon, she'll be beyond control. And you must make her ride with a saddle and gloves, or she'll be calloused all over."

Weariness and frustration honed Lanie's tongue. "If the horse doesn't mind, why should anyone else?"

"Where do you want these?" Ken inquired, as if oblivious of the family tension and friction around him.

"Upstairs, the first door to the left," Lanie replied. Her blue eyes flashed a warning signal to her mother. "Tell Maple to set another place. And serve wine."

"Are we celebrating something?"

"The red carpet welcome," Lanie said cryptically, preceding Kenneth Steele up the curved stairway down which, seventeen years before, in heirloom satin and lace, she had descended as Brian Hall's bride.

"I see you came back," the caretaker said sourly. "So who do I take orders from now, you or her?"

"Whoever issues them, Furbusher. Just do your job, and we won't have any problems with each other. Stay out of my way, and I'll try to stay out of yours."

"Yes, *sir*, Mr. Steele."

Ken wanted to punch the supercilious gnome-face. He'd seen rodents on the river docks and in the Irish Channel ghetto with that same expression. They used to pillage the pantry and sneak around in the house at night. His mother set traps for them, and he shot at them with B-B guns. He hated rats.

"Where you want your stuff, Mr. Steele?"

"Never mind. I'll take care of it."

"The servants coming back?"

"Eventually, I suppose. It's up to Mrs. Hall."

Ken left the watchdog on the threshold. The house still awed him as much, if not more, than the first time he had entered it. He wondered if he would ever get used to it enough to feel at home, comfortable. Lanie's attitude, her damnable procrastination, didn't help. Nor the old lady's condescension. Nor the girl's impertinence.

A few days later the youngest of the trio galloped up like one of the Furies on her mount, incensed to find him practicing on the putting green with one of her sire's golf clubs. Dismounting, she immediately demanded to know what he thought he was doing.

"What does it look like, pitching horseshoes?"

"Man, you've really moved in this time, haven't you? Bed, board, booze, and golf clubs!"

"All borrowed, Beth. It gets bloody boring and lonesome playing billiards and solitaire."

"There's a stock tank," she quipped, indicating the Olympic-size swimming pool. "Don't you swim?"

"So much I'm getting water-logged."

"And liquor-logged?"

"That, too," Ken conceded.

Beth relented, remembering how the isolation and loneliness of the estate had affected her. "Yeah, I reckon you could go flaky in this place. What do you say we bury the hatchet?"

"In whose back?"

She laughed, and it was the first time Ken had heard her laughter. Spontaneous, effervescent, delightful. Somehow he didn't think she could fake an emotion. Whatever she felt must be genuine, because her senses would not react to pretense or phoniness. "Oh, I hope it won't be that violent," she said. "I don't like violence. I don't like shams or masquerades, either. I like to be myself, and for other people to be themselves. Why don't you just be you?"

"I thought I was," Ken said.

"No, you're somebody else. I don't know who, but I think you're trying to be the person you think Mom and Grandma expect. I bet you spent half your life trying to be somebody else. Most people do, you know. They don't like or believe or trust what they are, so they form a new image and try to build a personality into it. They think they're discovering and establishing their identity, but they're wrong. It's not even human, any more than a statue is real. Just the old Pygmalion syndrome, that's all."

"You may be right," Ken said.

"No maybe. I am right, you'll see." She was emphatic. "Walk with me to the pavilion."

They crossed the terraced lawn to an outdoor entertainment area. Roofed concrete patio large enough for square dancing; two long barbecue pits, chairs, lounges, bright umbrellas. Bathhouses and cabanas beside the glistening blue-tiled pool, from which a handyman seemed to be perpetually removing leaves, either with a vacuum apparatus or long-handled net.

"Sit," Beth invited before a cypress bench. "I

think I have just the diversion for you, Mr. Steele. A safari in the Big Thicket."

"Trying to lose me, girl? I hear some people don't come out of that jungle."

"Don't worry. Mark's a skilled guide."

"I thought there was a catch," Ken said. "You expect to tag along, right?"

She grinned. "All the way."

"Without your mother's permission?"

"She'd never give it," Beth said petulantly.

Ken lit a cigarette. "Beth, you must know that'd bust me with her? Is that what you want?"

She begged a drag. Ken granted it. She blew a neat smoke ring. "Not if she didn't know anything about it. I'm only trying to help, Ken. You said you were bored, with nothing to do, and I know the feeling. It's killing. Sure I want to see Mark, be with him. But what the heck! Can't we trust each other that much?"

"Did you see Carradine while your mother was away?"

"We were in touch," Beth admitted.

"How?"

"Smoke signals, man."

"Bull, baby. You were together, and I mean *together.*"

"The way you and Mom were together in New Orleans?"

"That's a different proposition, Beth. Don't try to equate it."

"How different? The old double standard for adults and kids. Morality isn't figured that way in my mind."

"You left out one important factor," Ken said. "Love."

"And is that a privilege of maturity, too? How do you know Mark and I are not in love?"

"You're a child!"

"And you're making noises like a father already," Beth observed. "Mom, Grandma, and now you all monitoring me. I think I'll just split the whole lousy scene."

Placation was in order. "I'll think about that Thicket offer."

She smiled cynically. "You're bartering, aren't you? Trying to buy my cooperation."

"Maybe. Reciprocal trade agreement. You don't rock my boat with Lanie, and I won't tip your canoe with Mark." They shared the cigarette again. And then Ken touched the Indian beads around her neck. She had a lovely throat, smooth, richly tanned, and her head sat on it like a flower on a gracefully curved stem. Her beauty was inherent, natural, requiring no artificiality, and she employed none. "Your brave give you these pretty baubles?"

"They're love beads," she said. "Mark loves me."

"In spite of all your nasty wampum?"

"It's true, damn you!"

"Then why is he seeing you on the sly, knowing that your people resent him?"

"He doesn't know. I haven't told him."

"Beth, he doesn't have to be told. You know that. Unless he's a wooden Indian, he *knows*."

"We don't talk about it," she insisted. "Anyway, it's none of your business."

"It might be, eventually. And it can't work, Beth. You and an Indian? Be sensible."

"Grandma doesn't think it can work for you and Mom, and she tells her to be sensible."

"You keep drawing parallels," Ken said. "The situations are not the same, Beth. I'm not an Indian."

"You don't know what you are, man. At least Mark knows he's an Indian, and I know he's an Indian. He's not digging in ancestral burial mounds trying to locate tribal skeletons. He's descended from chiefs!"

"Bully for him."

Their alliance couldn't seem to solidify. Inadvertently one or the other breached it. And yet they shared a mutual desire for friendship. Beth wanted and needed him as an ally, as much as he wanted and needed her in his camp. She extended the olive branch again. "I'm sorry, Ken. Can't we compromise?"

"Sure, Beth. But no conspiracy, please. I mean, don't expect me to plot with you and Mark against your family. I couldn't do that. You understand, don't you?"

"I guess," she said, standing. "I'd better blow now, before the caretaker gets some wrong ideas and reports to Whitney House. I think he's a spy for Grandma. That's why I don't dare invite Mark here. Furbusher hates Indians. And Negroes. And Mexicans. And Jews. Everybody but himself. He'd have made a good Nazi."

Brute was nibbling on a boxwood, marring its clipped precision, which Beth knew would infuriate the caretaker, who also hated horses. Ken helped her mount. "Thanks for coming," he said. "You brightened my day."

She picked up the reins. "And you will think about the safari?"

"Yes," he promised. "How do you ride that beast without a saddle?"

"He lets me, that's how. I think because he can still feel free. Animals don't like bondage any more than people."

Ken gazed at her admiringly. Her youthful wisdom kept amazing him. "Mark's a lucky guy."

"You'll like him, Ken."

"Just remember. No deals."

"Oh, shit!" Beth swore lustily. "There you go again. All I want is for you to like him. Treat him right."

"Like the Big Chief," Ken said and knew he'd ruptured the treaty again. "Like a friend," he amended, slapping the horse because he wanted to spank the rider, and she was off in a cloud of red dust.

"Rides like an Injun, that kid," Farbusher declared with his annoying habit of sudden appearances and unsolicited comments. "A sight for any man's eyes."

"There're some leaves on the pool," Ken told him. "Skim 'em off. I want to take a dip."

"Cool off, eh? Yeah, it's hotter'n Hades, all right. The dog days here are the doggest. And pretty little gals like that don't make it no cooler, neither."

He grinned insidiously and sauntered off, not expecting a reply. One thing Ken knew: if ever he got authority over the estate employees, Furbusher would be the first to go.

Ken swam for an hour, trying to relax, hoping that Beth would forget about the proposed trek to the Thicket. He already knew what Lanie's reaction would be: explosive and annihilating. Too big a gamble to take with the mother to win the child. He'd just have to worm out of it somehow. And then Beth would consider him a coward, worthy of her contempt and scorn, and he'd never earn her trust and respect. His dilemma mounted, his problems pyramided.

But, dammit, he needed and wanted something

to do! What was he, a pet on the preserve? To run and fetch when Lanie snapped her fingers, rewarded with morsels of affection if he performed to her satisfaction and scolded if he didn't. Was that all she really wanted or expected of him? And was he supposed to just "sit pretty" while she tried to make up her mind whether to permanently leash him or not, one day yes, the next no, as if she were pulling hairs off his back.

He abandoned the pool abruptly, put on a robe, and went inside to write a letter.

The only stationery he could find in the library desk was personal, gray linen with black imprint for the late master, and white with royal blue English script for the mistress. Why not parchment scrolls and plumed quills and sealing wax! Ken removed a few sheets of the mourning-gray and black-inked the name at the top, taking some grim satisfaction in the obliteration. If only he could blot out Lanie's memories of her husband so easily, or his own of his wife. For Hall's ghost still haunted his castle, as Michele's did Halcyon.

He dated the letter and began:

"Dear Aunt Selma:

I wanted to have a long talk with you before leaving New Orleans, but there wasn't time. So much business to take care of, so many loose ends to tie up, since if all goes well here, I won't be returning except for a visit.

I gave up the lease on the apartment and had my belongings went to Halcyon. Gerald Howe, my partner, will either absorb or liquidate the firm.

It'll be an entirely new setup here, and I hope I can hack it. But the organization is much too vast and complex to describe, much less master, and I admit I have some qualms about entering it. So far, however, Mrs. Hall has not tried to involve me in any capacity, and I wonder if she is having misgivings about my ability and competence. I feel like a trainee under observation, who must serve an apprenticeship and pass muster before even being admitted to the ranks, much less through the portals of the upper echelon. I'm getting sensitive, in fact, about my total lack of involvement in anything. I have not met any of her friends or associates, and no date has been set for the official ceremony. I think the whole thing will hinge on the girl's acceptance or rejection of me, and I am trying now to win her confidence. I've given up on the old lady, who is another Madame Danielle. Apparently it is my fate, of course, to be challenged and thwarted and ostracized by grand dames!

I've put some money in Mother's account given you power of attorney. With Dad's union and Social Security pensions and Medicare, there should be enough to manage until I can provide more. But should an emergency arise for her or yourself, please let me know immediately, and I'll do what I can.

I wish you could see this place, Auntie. It's like something out of the *Arabian Nights*. Fantastic! Wealthy Texans are legendary for their flamboyance and eccentricity, but the one who built this palace in the pines must have been king and champion of them all. You must come for a visit when I become more than a pretender to the throne. Ironically, the heir apparent does not dote on the empire and has other ideas about her future, which her family would surely consider treasonous. Still the child has admirable courage and defiance, and I can't help wishing her mother were more like her. Taming the darling little shrew will present a challenge, and I am not at all sure such a delightfully free spirit can or should be tamed, broken, subdued.

For lack of other occupation, I think I shall resume my genealogical research. I'm afraid I'll continue to be regarded as a nonentity—indeed a trespasser by Dame Whitney and persona non grata in her realm until doomsday, unless I can establish a satisfactory heraldry. As I've said, she and Madame Danielle are similar in many respects, too many for my comfort.

Now I must close and get ready to visit the Queen, who is in expedient retreat at Whitney House. Becoming her consort would be quite an accomplishment requiring the hurdling of numerous obstacles—and ultimately I may fail. But I want her desperately and should hate to lose out through some default or technicality. Wish me luck, Aunt Selma, and pray that nothing goes wrong this time. Surely I can't be so unfortunate again. Surely the third time will be the charm.

Take care of yourself, dear, and kiss Mother for me. Love to you both, always,

Kenneth."

CHAPTER THIRTEEN

He would mail the letter on the way to Whitney House this evening. Until then he would read. He was surrounded by books, wall-to-wall; there should be some on the Big Thicket.

"What did you do today?" Lanie asked at the Rendezvous, Woodland's attempt at a romantic nightclub, featuring a cocktail lounge and tiny dance floor.

"Nothing much," he said. "What's to do?"

"Maybe it's time you met some people? How about a party? I'm dying to introduce you."

"To be appraised by the local hierarchy, under the watchful eyes of the dowagers? No, thanks. I had enough of that social protocol in New Orleans. Scrutinized in receiving lines by the Old Guard. I've heard that small-town society is more exclusive and circumspect than any other, by sheer virtue of its smallness."

"Not ours, darling. We go to Houston for the grand affairs—debut balls, symphonies, important functions. But we're just plain folk here. The Bucolic Barbecue Bunch. And some of us fox hunt in jeans and brush jackets."

"Do you?"

144

"No, I still prefer jodphurs and regulation coat—a habit I developed in finishing school in Virginia. Foxcroft."

"Why isn't Beth attending your alma mater? I thought that was traditional for mother and daughter?"

Lanie frowned. "You should know my daughter's opinion of tradition by now. I think it's her ambition in life to kick over all the traces."

"Maybe she just has different interests, Lanie?"

"Such as the Thicket Indians? She's also interested in the longhorn, whooping crane and ivory-billed woodpecker, among other vanishing species. The dinosaur and dodo would be alive and well and living in Texas today if my daughter could help it."

"What's wrong with that attitude?"

"Just don't agree with her that destroying trees is wrong," Lanie fumed, missing a step. "She's got a thing for trees too, you know. And I'm in the lumber business, remember. But Beth doesn't seem to understand why the whole country can't be one Big Thicket." She missed another beat, lost the rhythm completely, said she was tired and wanted to leave.

"We just got here," Ken protested.

"I don't care. I've had enough of this provincial little parlor. Let's go."

Ken bowed, "Your servant, ma'am."

"Oh, stop your mockery! Honestly, sometimes you're as bad as Beth." On the way to the car, she asked, "Why didn't you tell me she visited you today, Ken?"

"So Furbusher is the court spy?"

"Spy? What're you talking about? For your information, I called while Beth was there. No answer in the house. I tried the caretaker's number. He told me my daughter had just arrived, and the two of you were outside together, at the putting green or pool or somewhere. But nobody was 'spying' on anybody!"

"So what's the beef? You don't approve of her visits? I thought you wanted us to get better acquainted. How else is she ever going to accept me?"

"I just don't like her visiting you alone, Ken. It doesn't look right."

"To whom? The caretaker? The hired hands? There's no one else around, Lanie. What should I do the next time? Order her off her own property?"

"That's rationalization, Ken. You always try to simplify what you can't justify."

They were driving around the square in circles. The red sandstone buildings seemed to have risen out of the terra cotta earth to become part of its landscape, as natural and permanent as the surrounding hills. The Civil War hero might have evolved there on his bronze horse. The frame homes might have grown like the trees and gardens.

"Just what do you think I'm trying to justify, Lanie? Seducing her, perhaps?"

Astonished, Lanie cried furiously, "Why would you say such a thing—unless it *has* occurred to you?"

"Holy Jesus Christ, we're at it again! If you'll direct me out of this merry-go-round to a country lane, I'll show you whose seduction interests me—"

"Don't you ever think of anything but sex?"

He groaned, as if in pain. "You're castrating me."

Woods enclosed the town. All streets led into them, and logging roads criss-crossed. Ken picked one and reined the yellow sports car. But when he reached for her, Lanie shied away.

"We can't solve all our problems that way."

"We haven't solved any that way, Lanie. Have we?"

"I want to talk about my Daughter." She capitalized the word, and he caught the emphasis.

"What about your daughter?"

"I've told you before, Ken, she's different. Rash and impulsive. She's also imbued with idiotic ideologies, hunting some mythical thing in life, which she'll never find, because it doesn't exist. And I don't want you encouraging her to pursue this dream or illusion or whatever."

"Why should I encourage her?"

"Because you're pretty good at chasing rainbows and mirages yourself."

It was warm in the car, heated with rising tempers. Ken opened his door for ventilation. Pines towered a hundred feet and more above and around them. He felt like a stunted growth in the shadows of giants. Lanie was only a silhouette beside him, almost indistinguishable, and beginning to seem like the most nebulous and evasive will-o'-the-wisp of all.

"What're you afraid of, Lanie? That I'll treat Beth as my own child, love her as much as her father did, and maybe she'll respond? And you'd be jealous of that kind of relationship? You could dissolve that fear easily enough in marriage, if you harbor it, by pregnancy."

"You're obsessed with the idea of impregnation," she accused. "Why, for God's sake? Do you doubt your virility?"

"Dorene had two abortions," he said darkly.

"And you let her?"

"I didn't know until afterwards. She was a sly bitch, in more ways than one."

"How do you know you were responsible? If she was so flagrantly unfaithful, anyone in Fort Dix could have been guilty?"

"Not the first year," he said.

"Well, I can't honestly blame her, Ken. To bear or not to bear should be every woman's innate privilege. But it's ironic that you should latch on to three such reluctant reproducers, isn't it? That's enough to frustrate any male chauvinist, I suppose. The inferior female rejecting the almighty male seed is bound to decimate his ego and give him a phallus-complex."

Ken drummed his fingers on the steering wheel. "You don't want a husband, Lanie, or father for Beth. You don't even want a lover except sporadically. You've got more hangups than a country school cloakroom, and you're driving me loco. But I won't submit to complete mutilation, no matter the rewards. I won't let you grind me into sawdust, compress me to pulp, and cast me off as a by-product. And I won't be just a piece of dead wood in your Mill, either."

"You expect to be Chairman of the Board?"

"I expect to be more than a stick."

"Were you a wheel in the Danielle organization?"

"I pulled my share of the load, Lanie, and maybe more. I functioned as a man, not a eunuch, although Michele did her best to emasculate me."

"Oh, you poor darling," Lanie mocked. "Constantly tortured by cruel females. Hall Industries has managed to move on its own power for many years, Ken. But an appropriate position will be found for you when the time comes."

More finger tapping, louder. Evidently she was unaware of the implication in her words. "And what would you consider an appropriate position for the son of a stevedore and seamstress, Mrs. Hall?"

"One commensurate with your talents and ability, darling. But first things first. I think a barbecue would be nice, don't you?"

"Barbecue?" The abrupt transition stupified him.

"For the introductory bash, dear. Something rural and informal, since you object to formality so much. Just a few close friends and business associates, I should think. Is there someone in particular you'd like to invite from home? There are plenty of guest rooms, you know. Only let's wait another month or so, shall we, until the weather's cooler? We have an absolutely beautiful autumn here—"

Ken started the motor, racing it impatiently. "I would like to invite a few people, Lanie. Aunt Selma. My partner, Jerry Howe. And Paul Chandre."

"Chandre?" She treated that as a whimsy. "Well, I suppose you have your reasons. But do you think your aunt is strong enough to travel? She seems so frail."

"Would you rather exclude her?"

"Oh no, of course not! I was just concerned for the poor dear's health. And your mother being left alone and all."

"Sure, I understand. Maybe we'd better spare Aunt Selma the ordeal. However, there is one other person I've just remembered and would like to include. A young man."

"Who?"

"Mark Carradine."

"Carradine? I never heard you mention that name before. Is he a relative?"

"No, I don't even know him, personally. But I think we should, Lanie, both of us."

"Why? Is he important?"

"That depends, I think, entirely on your definition of importance," Ken said.

CHAPTER FOURTEEN

The letter from New Orleans arrived Registered Special Delivery. Ken opened the legal-size envelope expecting to find a sheaf of bills accumulated by his mother. Instead there were many sheets of thin cheap stationery written in Aunt Selma's precise penmanship and pedantic English, plus a smaller sealed envelope with the notation "Read letter first."

"My Dear Nephew:

Yours of August 11th received, and please know that I have debated the prudence and effect of this answer a great deal in my mind and dreaded it in my heart, hoping that it would never be necessary. I realize now, however, that it was not only inevitable but compulsory and long overdue.

Unfortunately, your father, whose filial duty this was, chose to ignore it, and your poor mother is incapable of assuming it now, for she sinks deeper into oblivion every day. Thus, the responsibility devolves on me, and I must not shirk it. For I fear, dear boy, you are about to make another tragic marital mistake, and conscience compels me to do what I can to avert it. You should never have been allowed to

marry anyone in ignorance of your heritage.
And marriage with Lanine Whitney Hall
would, I feel, be as doomed as that with
Michele Chandre Danielle. For in due time
her family might investigate yours (if indeed
they are not already doing so!), as Michele's
undoubtedly did. And I still believe the Danielles had either discovered the truth, or were
on the verge of it, when the accident occurred.

Now I shall prolong your suspense no longer.

That journal, Kenneth, is not this family's.
The hand is not either of your paternal great-
grandparents. Neither Matthew nor Sybil could
read or write. They were slaves, and the diary
belonged to their master, whose surname they
assumed when the river plantation was sacked
and burned during the Civil War. Matthew was
black, pure African, and a fieldhand. But Sybil
was a young mulatto, Steele's daughter by one
of his slaves, and maid to the mistress of the
house, a situation not uncommon in those days.

Matthew and Sybil fled the plantation during
the chaos, taking the journal with them, hiding
and living in the swamps for awhile, eventually working their way across the Sabine River
to lower East Texas. They took refuge in a
dense forest, where with the help of some
friendly Indians they lived primitively until
the war was over. Then they found work on a
cotton plantation, where their son Virgil was
born. At eighteen Virgil came to New Orleans, met and eventually married a young
mulatto, Clio Dewar. Clio was Jamaican and
very beautiful, light-skinned, exquisitely fea-
tured. Your father and I were the issues of this
union and could 'pass,' whatever that means. I

152

used to wonder. Pass for what? A human being?

At any rate, delivered by midwives with no birth certificates to betray our color, we were judged on appearance alone and able to attend white schools. Our parents worked very hard and sacrificed much to educate us. Your father was a high school senior and I in my third year of college when we lost Papa of a coronary. Pneumonia took Mama five years later, and so you never knew either of your paternal grandparents. A pity, for they were wonderful people.

After graduation, Joseph went to work on the docks. I continued in college until I received my degree. I wanted to teach. I had a naïve and burning dedication: 'Better to light one candle than to curse the darkness.' Racism became my crusade, my obsession, and I pursued it diligently and doggedly for as long as possible in the South of forty years ago. Needless to say, this was not productively long. Advocating racial equality then (and even now) was heresy and treason to the system of White Supremacy. The immediate penalty was reprimand, followed by suspension, and ultimate expulsion from the public schools, as a poisonous plant which must be eradicated from the garden, lest its pollen disseminate and contaminate the flowers.

I could not practice my profession, except in a privately endowed institution for retarded children, where presumably I could do no 'harm.' It was 'safe' for me to mingle with those poor blighted blossoms of nature, whose simple minds were incapable of absorbing my 'liberal

poisons' and equally pointless for me to at-
to inject them. Resentment fostered frustration,
resolution degenerated into futility. One must
live, and political ideology and social con-
formity were the criteria in the segregated
culture of my day. Perhaps I was a coward
taking the path of least resistance, but one can
endure and survive only so much disillusion
and despair and defeat, before noble incentive
and inspiration dissolve in ignoble impotence
and dissipate in recreant surrender. Finally, a
form of mental and spiritual decay sets in
which, God forbid and forgive, passes for
resignation and even contentment.

Meanwhile, your father Joseph had chosen
a different and less rocky route. While hunting
a Mardi Gras costume in a shop in the Quarter,
he found a wife—a sweet little spinster from
the Red River Valley, who had a knack with
needle and thread. They had a country wedding
at her home, and a year later you were born
right here in the Irish Channel. The way such
blood mixtures are measured in our society,
this makes you a quadroon, one quarter Negro.
But I've considered you exceptionally handsome, as such racial blendings frequently are,
and believe it would be virtually impossible for
anyone to guess your lineage.

Nevertheless, as you surely know, your father
could not legally contract marriage in this or
any other Southern State, where miscegenation
laws still prevail. The union could have been
declared null and void and its offspring illegitimate. The same is true in Texas, of course,
where marriage is forbidden between a Caucasian and a person of as little as one eighth

Negro blood. The constitutionality of these laws is being tested, and they may eventually be repealed, but at present they are still on the books. Whatever the ultimate outcome, I believe that Mrs. Hall should be apprised of the facts and allowed to make her own decision. Marriage under any other circumstances would constitute fraud, Kenneth, and grounds for annulment in any and all fifty states. You wed Dorene Granato and Michele Danielle ignorant of your ancestry and against my advice to your father to inform you. If you wish to wed Lanine Hall in defiance of it, that must be your prerogative. But I think honor and integrity and justice demand your honesty in the matter, son.

So look no more in the white cemeteries of East Texas or anywhere else for your 'lost' ancestors. The graves of Matthew and Sybil Steele lie in the 'nigger patch' of the Bolden Plantation adjoining Woodland County. But they are unidentifiable, the wood crosses long since rotted away, the ruined property returned to forestland, reclaimed by nature.

If you are wondering if your mother were aware of all this, be assured that she was, although not from the beginning. Your father kept it from her until her first pregnancy. By the time you were born, she had accepted and adjusted to it, although she never dared inform her poor but fanatically proud white countryfolk. I do not think she ever worried seriously until the inquest into Michele's death. And then she was beset with an almost irrational fear that the truth would somehow emerge from the shadows and destroy you, and undoubtedly the strain and anxiety contributed to her massive stroke.

Now you know, Kennie, and I can only hope that you are grateful for knowing. At least I have spared you the ordeal of a possible surprise discovery, than which there is nothing more cruel and unforgivable, and perhaps also an unexpected confrontation with Mrs. Hall. For even my brief observation of her suggests that she would not take such a revelation lightly. No doubt she considers herself a person of quality; I cannot visualize her marrying you in possession of the knowledge or remaining with you upon discovery.

I can only hope and trust that you understand my motives and realize that I have acted in your best interests. You've had enough marital strife and unhappiness; it would break my heart to see you suffer more, and I would blame myself, feeling derelict in duty and conscience. For whether or not you acknowledge your people publicly, Kenneth, I think you must at least own them to yourself. Otherwise, you are less than the man I have always considered you.

Your Devoted Aunt,
Selma

P.S.

No doubt you have guessed that the additional envelope contains the missing pages of the journal, plus those written in French, which I myself removed and translated long ago. You will see that they were entries of the French mistress of Mystic Plantation and concerned household affairs, and the names of Matthew and Sybil appear, along with those of other slaves.

I do not know why they took the record when they left. Perhaps they believed it contained their vital statistics or other personally important information. Possibly, even though illiterate, they recognized it as a valuable social and historic document, something negotiable to pass on to their children, aware that they would possess few other assets. You be the judge of its worth and significance, dear.

S."

He was numb, at first, unable to assemble and react, as if he'd been struck a severe blow to the head. He used to wonder about the emotional impact upon a person suddenly confronted with an unexpected reality about himself—that he was illegitimate, or sexually perverted, or insane, or the child of a criminal. The initial shock would naturally be stunning, the repercussions devastating.

Nigger.

He'd heard the word all his life, had grown up with it in his ears and frequently on his lips, spoken both in condescension and contempt, for even the poorest white trash in the Channel ghetto considered themselves above the blacks. It was an everyday fact of life in his segregated childhood. And if colored people were regarded as inferior, their blood mixtures were even more so. Mulattoes, for instance, had lived in a kind of pathetic social no man's land, ostracized and often abhorred by both races, segregating themselves in colonies around Leonville, near Opelousas, and Isle Brevele on the Cane River. Quadroons mingled more freely but even they were taboo in the better homes, except as domestics.

His 'passing' father had worked on the docks with blacks, but he had not eaten with them in restaurants or drunk with them in bars, and his son had not played with them, or gone to school with them, or sat in movies or on buses with them. Big Joe Steele had black eyes and ruddy skin burned by the semitropical sun, and coarse features but not classically Negroid. He resembled any number of crude, muscular bayou or backwoods men who lived by the sweat of brawn and brow.

In a city of dark eyes and cafe au lait complexions, Selma Steele was just another native. But Ken wondered now if her race had kept her single as much as her career. God, how ironic and frustrating it must have been teaching the imperfect progeny of the "superior race" in that segregated institution how to build block skyscrapers and color pictures of whites in gracious homes and gardens, where the black faces were always on servants and handymen. He had painted many such scenes himself in art class in school and studied the carefully biased history of slavery in the approved textbooks, in which the system was defended as economically prudent and all masters and mistresses were depicted as kind and generous and solicitous of their chattels' welfare.

And so not even his surname was his own, but borrowed—stolen, in fact. What was the poor devil called when they captured him in that African jungle and shipped him in chains to be auctioned off the slave block? Some unpronounceable tribal name—Umbago or Wambuzi or something? Had he been naked and weirdly painted, with bushy hair and a bone in his nose and a necklace of leopard teeth? And his master, the man who had bought him like a wild animal to be tamed by whip if necessary, was a Christian, so he'd given the savage a Christian name. Matthew, after the apostle? That was kind of Mr. Steele. Oh, there was a lot of the milk of human kindness in Monsieur Steele! He'd poured some of it into his female darkies and begotten a mulatto daughter, who became wife of Matthew. Merci, Monsieur. Merci beaucoup, you goddamn slave-fucking sonofabitch! Nigger!

Had the suspicious Danielles ultimately discovered the facts, as Selma suspected? And had Michele taken her betrayal of the family sovereignty seriously when Maman revealed their disgrace? No disgrace to engage in incest—that was a sovereign privilege and old Chandre tradition. But to marry the great-grandson of slaves! Michele was dramatic, unstable, hopelessly in love with her uncle; an untenable situation which she had never successfully reconciled or compromised, merely endured. It was not inconceivable that she had cut that tow rope herself, committing "accidental suicide" rather than risk public scandal in a divorce or annulment, which still would not enable her to marry her lover.

Now there was Lanine Whitney Hall, WASP supreme, with a mother even more fanatically genealogy conscious, if that was possible, than the French Catholic Madame Danielle. And Lanie's little white moonchild stuck on an Indian—and nobody aware of the nigger in the woodpile.

The phone was persistently ringing. Beth was supposed to call. Ken laughed, choked on the laughter, picked up the receiver.

"Yassuh?"

"Ken?"

"It's me, honeychile."

"Well, stop clowning. I thought one of the servants was back. Are we going to the Thicket tomorrow?"

"I don't think so, Beth."

"You promised!"

"I promised to think about it," he corrected.

"You're afraid," she accused. "Afraid of Mom and
Grandma . . . and your own shadow! You're a
coward, and I despise cowards."

"I'll go," Ken relented. Why not? What did he
have to lose now?"

"You will? Honest?"

"Honest Injun."

Static hummed on the wire. "I don't like cracks
like that."

"Sorry, baby. I forgot."

"It's okay. I forgive you. Listen carefully, now.
We have to leave bright and early. Wear some old
clothes and comfortable shoes—boots, if you got
any with you. I'll take a couple of canteens of
water."

"Just for the record, what'll you tell Mommy?"

"That I'm going to ride Silver all day, hi-ho."

"No mention of Tonto?"

She froze again.

"Beth, are you there?"

"I'm here," she thawed. "You know the stable
where I keep Brute?"

"I think so. It's on a dead-end road, isn't it?"
Somehow that seemed to symbolize his life. Had
he possessed a coat of arms, it would surely include
a cul de sac. "Shall I meet you there?"

"No, at the crossroads near it. From there we can
take some backroads and logging lanes out of town.
Seven-thirty sharp, okay?"

"Okay," Ken agreed.

They were friends again. "Thanks, Dad."

Dad. It sounded good, felt good, until he realized the barriers to reality. Maybe if he just burned the letter and forgot it? No, fire would only destroy words on paper and substitute self-deception and denial. He took the evidence upstairs and locked it in his flight bag.

"It was strange to find a child there, a babe in the woods, yet less lost than her elders."
AN EVANGELIST'S HANDBOOK

CHAPTER FIFTEEN

As usual, when she thought she was beguiling her keepers, Beth was a blithe spirit. "How, man?"

"How yourself," Ken said, opening the door for her.

She hopped in, canteens swung jauntily over her shoulders, hair smoothly braided. Long-sleeved shirt with the tails out, faded denims, digger boots. Eyes glowing behind big round blue-colored glasses, while smoked ones shaded Ken's. She carried a brown paper sack.

"Mark doesn't want us to meet him on the reservation."

"Why not?"

"Oh, there might be a rumble if we didn't return on time. Sheriff, Rangers, dogs—the whole bit. I'm a VIP in these parts, you know. I hate it, but that's how it is, see. So we'll meet him on a road south of the reservation. I know the one, I'll direct you."

"Whatever he thinks best," Ken agreed. "But are you sure he knows the Thicket, Beth?"

"Nobody knows the Big Thicket completely, Ken. It was like three million acres before civilization whittled it down to three hundred thousand. Progress with its lousy stinking oil wells, pipe lines, logging operations. Destroying trees, wildlife, polluting streams with chemicals and salt water. Mark says their minister compares the developers to Ahab ruining Naboth's vineyard in the First Book of Kings. I compare them to criminals ravishing the earth and am sorry and ashamed to admit that my father was one of them." She winced, as if biting into a green persimmon. "Anyway, Mark won't take us to the parts he doesn't know. I buzzed him yesterday from a booth to set this up. He's waiting for us now, on the road I mentioned."

"I want to be back in Woodland before dark, Beth. Otherwise the game is over for both of us— you realize that, don't you?"

"Sure. Mom'll sack you and sock me and probably make heap big trouble for Mark. But let's not worry yet, huh? Let's just float free and easy and enjoy. I dig your outfit, man. Big White Hunter on safari. All you need is a Hemingway hat with leopard band, or British pith helmet."

More like platter lips and pierced nose, Ken thought; a black bearer with a back bundle.

"Yeah, that's all I need to be king of the jungle," he said. "You look pretty camp yourself."

Beth grinned comradely. "I feel like a conspirator, but it's fun. It's gonna be a blast living with you, Dad. I mean, having you around permanently."

"That may never happen, Beth. The parent part, that is. Especially not after this episode."

"Cheer up! If Mom doesn't marry you, I will when I'm older, even if I have to commit bigamy. Because I'm going to marry Mark, you know."

The sweet child. And now it was a double deception, mother and daughter, and doubly wrong; could lead to no end of complications. But what the hell! They were out for adventure today, an experience to remember. One thing at a time. Shove tomorrow, which might never come, and the future, which for all practical purposes was already behind him, lost centuries ago, when some remote relative ascended the gangplank of the first American-bound slave ship.

Mark Carradine was waiting, a tall bronzed young man with unmistakable features. He could never "pass" for anything but what he was, and Ken envied him his identity, his advantage over his enemies. Nobody could slap a genetic surprise on this boy in the midstream of life, rock his social boat precariously and possibly dash it on the great race-barrier reef. Nor could he be lured, beguiled, by the siren dream-song of some martyred latter-day Uncle Saint Tom hauled to his grave like so much drayage in a mule-drawn wagon. Whatever Little Wolf accomplished, he'd do alone and aware of the odds. And what would that be? Except for a miracle, what chance did an Indian have to be anything but an Indian? Less opportunity even than the Negro in the nitty-gritty of white society. But at least the red man knew where he stood in that world, which was more than Kenneth Steele knew at the moment. This bewildered brother was neither black nor white, and didn't even know his real name.

The Indian appraised him critically, as his ancestors might have appraised a prospective white trader of whom they were inherently suspicious, tentatively shaking hands before entering the car and removing his pack. And yet, ironically, one of Carradine's relatives may have been among the friendly tribe who had helped a pair of runaway slaves from Louisiana.

"Set the course," Ken told him. "You're the guide."

"Yeah, your genuine Indian scout. Little Wolf. Something to write on the postcards home. Got a loaded camera, to shoot me for the family album? Down this road a mile or so, man. I'll tell you when."

Almost immediately they were swallowed up in a seemingly endless hollow of green, with only a narrow strip of metallic blue sky visible above. A thoroughfare of some vintage, constructed by the lumber engineers, devastated by greed and profit, abandoned by progress to weeds and erosion but still passable.

"Stop here," Mark ultimately directed. "Pull off to the side and lock the chariot. Some poachers may be around."

Ken hesitated to leave the car, the known for the unknown. He had only to retrace the road to reach civilization again. God knew where this unchartered trail led. And Beth's sudden apprehensive silence indicated she'd never experienced the Thicket interior before either, with Mark Carradine or anyone else. Probably a guided tour on the reservation was the extent of her knowledge and experience, and so they were both neophytes, dependent on a boy far from his familiar surroundings, who may or may not be competent. A naïve young girl in love could be forgiven such trusting idiocy, but what was his excuse? Temporary insanity induced by shock?

"Watch for snakes," Mark cautioned, as they entered a narrow footpath. "Some deadly ones in here. Smoke if you like, sir—it'll help keep mosquitoes and other pests away. Just don't start any fires. What's for grub, Beth?"

"Cookies and raisins."

"That all? Why didn't you pick up something?"

"We left town too early, and I didn't want to

arouse Mom's suspicion by snitching from home. But we won't starve, Mark. It's only for one day, you know. We're not going to camp."

"Well, I put some jerky in my pack, anyway, compliments of one of your generous sportsmen last season. Grandfather cured it. The hunter didn't want the deer, just the pleasure of killing it and the antlers for his den. Christ, what some men won't do for a lousy trophy!"

Ken asked, "Were you the guide?"

"One of them—there were several. It was a hunting party from a Houston game club. Executive types. Trap shooting champions—you probably know the breed. The kind that hate to rough it in camp or anywhere else and let flunkies do all the hard and dirty work. The guides did everything but carry them piggyback. One of them was downed by dysentery the first day out, and it was a mess. Another got so jittery the night a skunk sprayed his tent, he let fly himself in his sleepingbag." He grinned cynically. "Real brave hombres."

Ken was embarrassed for Beth until he heard her laugh, sharing the Indian's mirthful memory. Oh, he was uptight, all right! Angry as a wounded buffalo about something, and trying for Beth's sake not to show it. And she was obviously wrapped up in this red boy with a face like a primitive wood carving, flint-hard body, and the personality of an arrow. Ken didn't want to come into conflict with him, but already they were off to less than a congenial start.

Following the leader even single file was difficult where the undergrowth encroached on the path, and Ken wondered how far they could go before it disappeared entirely in brush. "Shouldn't you be marking the trail, Guide?"

"I am, mentally and instinctively, man. An oak, sycamore, gum, sweet bay, magnolia—they're all markers if you know how to use 'em."

"Hell, Mark. Trees all look alike after awhile. In fact this whole country looks alike to me. Just one big bush! If you lose us in here, it'll be your hide, boy, when her folks lean on you."

"They'd have to find me first," he said sullenly. "This is my territory, you know, and it's no longer open season on Indians." He slashed an impeding plant with the sturdy stick he carried. "We were here first, long before the Spaniards, French, Mexicans, and Yankees. My people were guiding yours back in Sam Houston's time."

"I'm not a Texan," Ken said.

"Neither was Sam Houston, nor most of their other famous heroes, for that matter. They all came from other places, other lands. And they all trespassed, plundered, raped, murdered."

Beth meditated, "So did the Indians, Mark. And you know your tribe came from Tennessee to Texas in 1795. The Caddoes were already in their vicinity then, and before them the Basket Makers and other aborigines."

"All Indians, though. That's my point, Beth. We had villages all over North America long before your pioneers and frontiersmen 'settled' it."

"Oh, Mark—everyone knows Indians were on Plymouth Rock when the *Mayflower* landed." Picking up a stick of her own, she whacked impatiently at the undergrowth, telling Ken, "Don't mind Mark. Ever so often he regurgitates some stale Indian porridge. What he says is true, though. He knows his Texas history."

"Apologizing for me and my people, Beth?"

"No, of course not, Mark. But things aren't so

bad on the reservation any more, are they? I know they were terrible once, but there've been some improvements."

"Sure, and how long did it take? How many of us had to die of disease and starvation before anyone gave a damn? And why did we have to be herded into a compound in the first place, penned up like animals and forgotten for a hundred years? Not only in Texas but all over the country. So now we have some freedom and independence and self-respect—but we paid one helluva big price for it! And we'll go on paying. But when you have nothing, anything is an improvement, and you're grateful."

"I know, Mark—and you know how I feel about it. I'm on your side. But Ken doesn't know we play harmoniously on the racial seesaw and will think we're quarreling. Besides, he may be your step-father-in-law, so try to make a better impression."

"You're dreaming, baby. Hallucinating."

"Oh, hush. We came in here to see the Thicket. Show it to us."

"Just look, it's all around you."

"I mean the rare plants. The orchids and pitcher plants that eat insects and the ferns growing in trees."

"You've seen all that in your nature study and botany field trips."

"But Ken hasn't."

Mark indicated the hairy crotch of a hoary oak. "There's a good fern specimen. I don't think there's an orchid bog near, and many of the pitcher plants have been ruined by chemical sprays. Maybe we're lucky some trees are still left. Probably won't be in ten, or twenty years, the rate they're being destroyed."

A few small animals observed them shyly from the shadows. Birds continually sang, chirped, whistled, cackled, mourned, mocked. They saw some egrets, pure white, majestically plumed. A few great blue herons, four feet high, magnificent. A pair of spoonbills. Three water turkeys. And an almost extinct bald eagle. All threatened by poachers, pollution, and progress.

When they came upon an old hunters' campsite, Mark suggested a rest. A creek seeming to float a garden of purple water hyacinths ran near. Trees, mostly yellow pine, circled the twenty foot clearing.

"Beautiful!" cried Beth before she saw the moldering garbage heap on the edge. Bean and beer cans, paper dishes and towels, a curling deer hide and the pelts and bones of rabbits and squirrels and foxes, and nature struggling to hide the whole hideous mess with vegetation.

"The Nimrods do almost as much damage as the Ahabs," Mark said disgustedly. "And they don't bother to camouflage it, either. The Indians usually buried their refuse in middens—those prized mounds that archaeologists explore now. But I haven't seen many white men bury their debris in the wilderness. Too bad, because their successors won't have anything to study when they finally make themselves extinct."

Ken asked, "How far in are we?"

"Couple of miles or so. Think you could find your way back?" He was smoothing out some pine needles for Beth to sit on, like a straw mat, with him beside her.

"Probably not. You can test me on the return."

"You'd fail, man. We crossed scores of trails. You could wander on any of them for days, weeks, even months. You're lost. Without me, you could die in here."

"And Beth with me?"

Mark looked at the girl with different eyes—profound as still black water too deep to fathom. Only the surface glimmer betrayed him. "No," he said softly, "I wouldn't want to lose her."

"So you're the superior man in the Thicket," Ken conceded, settling himself against a pine trunk.

"Only in the Thicket?"

Examining a woodchip as if he'd picked it off Carradine's shoulder, Ken said, "I'm not interested in scratching your heritage lice, Indian. I've got enough of my own. Understand?"

"Me savvy."

"And knock off that Hollywood Indian dialog. You speak English well enough."

"Mark's a brain," Beth said proudly. "He graduated from high school with honors. I want him to go to college and study Business Administration."

Obviously she thought there was a future for him in Hall Industries, and Ken could imagine her family's reaction. Poor little rich girl. Didn't she realize she could start her own Indian war?

"What does Mark want?"

"The same thing, I hope."

"Any objections, sir?" from Mark.

"No, just some advice for both of you," Ken replied. "Wait a few more years and see how you feel then."

"Grow up, you mean, and we'll grow apart? What are you, the family hatchetman sent to chop me down?"

"Don't be so defensive, Mark."

"Defensive? I'm proud of my ancestry. At least I'm all Indian, not some sorry duke's mixture like

173

so many of your breed. I'm pure Coushatta with some chief stock. How pure is your blood and how far back can you trace it? You'll find more ethnic mongrels in your tribe than mine, I guarantee."

"No doubt," Ken ruefully agreed. "And while we're on the subject, would you marry a white woman?"

"Would a white woman marry me?" Mark countered, avoiding Beth's anxious eyes. "Would she want half-breed kids? And would her social code, or that of her 'chiefs' permit it? At any rate, she'd know what she was up against. It wouldn't be like walking blind into an ambush."

Beth sipped quietly from her canteen. She knew much of Mark's hostility was pretense to disguise humility. He'd been out in the white world long enough to have developed his share of cynicism and wariness. His athletic prowess made him a hero in the sports arena, but it was not easy to preserve the image and illusion away from it. And he was keenly aware of the unrelated competitions and challenges he alone would have to meet and conquer, or lose.

The high-noon sun blazed fiercely overhead, concentrating on the shadeless area. Beth longed to crawl into the cool dim recesses with Mark. They had been together intimately only once, while her mother was in New Orleans. She had sent Mark an urgent message, and he'd promptly responded. He had caught a bus to town, and she'd ridden her horse to meet him in the peripheral woods of Hall Estate safe from the caretaker's scrutiny. It was embarrassing at first, and frustrating, and that was when she had realized how little books could teach about things which had to be experienced. But they had managed, determined, and succeeded in making it worthwhile and even beautiful. Now all she wanted was another opportunity, another beautiful experience, another chance to prove she loved him.

Ken offered Mark a cigarette. "Smoke?"

"The Camel calumet, huh?" Mark shrugged and accepted and shared Ken's lighter.

"I think I know how you feel, Mark."

"About what?"

"The things that bug you."

"I doubt it. Like you said, we all have our own lice to scratch. And only people of the same skin can know all its itches. You're not in my hide, so you can't possibly know about my particular bugs, or feel or care too much if I scratch myself raw and bloody."

"Grind your tomahawk, Indian, and collect your emotional scalps. But our little powwow here won't solve anything, you know, and it does seem a shame not to enjoy all this peace and serenity. Especially since the Thicket's one of the last refuges left to man in this country, and I understand even it's vanishing."

"Thanks to technology," Mark nodded. "The bulldozer is the most destructive implement ever invented. It's wiping out fifty and more acres of Thicket every day. This goddamn steel-jawed monster has already chewed up two and a half million acres. Some thousand-year-old trees have been splintered. Whole rookeries of egrets and herons have been sprayed with poison, killed in the nest and even in the egg. Why? To make room for profitable pines to grow. They use every form of violence and power and destruction. Chemicals, dynamite, fire, oil, salt, machines, guns."

"Ken hasn't destroyed anything here, Mark," Beth said. "He didn't invent the bulldozer or rifle or dynamite or DDT. And you don't have to remind me that my old man was an Ahab, you know. I'm well aware of it."

"Sorry, baby. I just get carried away sometimes."

Ken stood, brushing his clothes. "Hadn't we better hit the trail again, Mark? Beth is here without her mother's knowledge, and I want her home before dark. I'm responsible for her."

"Since when?" Mark scowled.

"Since I agreed to this outing in a weak moment." Squinting at the sun-glare, "Wish I had a cold beer."

"Wish I'd filled my canteen with wine," Beth said.

"What, and corrupt this poor Indian with firewater?" But he said it without rancor, with humor even, and Beth relaxed and smiled at him. Some camaraderie might just possibly emerge and develop, after all.

CHAPTER SIXTEEN

The Thicket sought to defend its sanctuary with formidable natural barriers, so that merely maneuvering in the "tight-eye" understory became a challenge and endurance a feat. The intruders were scratched by brush, pricked by thorny brambles, slapped by tenacious branches, entangled in vicious vines. Sweat drenched both men, and Ken panted with the effort. Beth's shirt was pasted to her wet body, outlining her braless breasts. What little makeup she had worn had vanished, leaving only the pink flushed sheen of moisture; and her long braids, tortured by limbs and twigs, hung limp and ragged on her shoulders. She felt as if she'd run a ruthless, relentless kangaroo court. Moreover, Mark's preoccupation for the past hour generated a sinking suspicion that he was not certain of their location.

Ken, also intent and largely silent, seemed to share her apprehension. Finally, approaching an unfamiliar grove of scrub palmetto that appeared hopelessly impenetrable, he abruptly halted and demanded, "Mark, where the devil are we? I thought we were going out?"

"*Quien sabe, senior?*"

"You better *sabe*, Indian, and fast."

"Let me get my bearings," Mark said, sobering, and Beth's heart dropped like a lead anchor in her chest.

"Well?" Ken insisted impatiently.

"Now don't panic, folks," Mark calmly urged. "I'll figure it out. Just keep quiet and let me think."

They waited for what seemed like a sojourn in limbo, while Mark reconnoitered, craning his neck vainly, obviously disoriented and dismayed.

"I knew it," Ken muttered. "You're screwed up, right? We're lost in this goddamn bush! Can't we backtrack? Get out your compass."

"Wouldn't help," Mark said, "even if I had one."

"You don't have a compass?"

"Don't own me. A good instrument is expensive, and a bad one is worse than none at all. I'm just a poor Indian."

"Oh, brother! A guide without a compass."

"Wouldn't help, anyway," Mark repeated. "We've turned around too many times, and we're too deep in the interior. Could go in the wrong direction, no matter which we chose."

"What do you mean, we? You're the smartass Indian guide. Knew it all a few hours ago, strutting and crowing like a red rooster. Well, if you've fouled up on this, Carradine, I'm going to pluck your tail feathers!"

Mark squirmed, as embarrassed as a young brave who had bungled his puberty rites and failed his manhood test before the maiden he had hoped to impress and capture for squaw. He scratched his head. "First, we got to avoid these palmettos. Might be acres of them."

"Good reasoning," Ken said cynically, "especially since I wasn't about to let you drag us through that obstacle course."

The green fans clacked like hundreds of mocking tongues, gleeful at having confused and rejected the invaders.

"I saw a baygall through the trees about fifty yards back," Mark recalled. "Might be another hunters' camp."

Ken asked, "Did you say bagel?"

"No, every tourist makes that stale crack. A baygall's a seepage pond, so named because bay trees flourish on its banks. There're some huge baygalls in the Thicket, but that was a little one I glimpsed."

"Well, lead the way," Ken growled.

"Don't be mad at Mark," Beth placated. "He didn't lose us purposely, Ken."

"What difference does that make? Your mother's going to skin me alive."

"Is that all you're worried about, your own hide?"

"Yours too, Beth. And Mark's. We're not exactly on a field trip with an eagle scout, you know. Nor the Three Wise Men to be guided by a star in the East. We're lost in a wilderness!"

It was a small pond, and uninviting except to cottonmouth moccasins. A gray cypress skeleton, boney-kneed and empty-armed, stood like a ghostly sentinel on a knoll waiving tatters of moss. And in the nearby clearing, the previous nomads had left their usual souvenirs.

"It's almost four now," Ken said, consulting his watch. "Even if we knew the way out and started immediately, we couldn't possibly hack it by dark. Could we, Mark?"

"No way, man."

"All right, then. Let's sit down and study the situation. Unfortunately nobody else knows we came here, unless you had the good sense to tell someone on the reservation? No, your whipped warrior's expression answers that question. And I stupidly allowed Beth to swear me to secrecy. You're both too young to know better, but I should bey lynched."

"Probably will be," Beth predicted somberly, "before Mom and Grandma finish with you. Provided the buzzards don't get us first."

"Don't talk that way," Mark said, "even in fun."

"Who's funning?"

All the stories she'd heard and read about the Big Thicket since childhood suddenly culminated in her own predicament. Tales of horror, mostly, about endless wandering and eventual insanity and death. Some victims had been discovered ravaged and raving like lunatics, or reverted to primitiveness, naked and wild. Others were never found at all, their souls said to be eternally roaming, for the Thicket abounded in mystery and superstition. The natives all knew of the haunted Ghost Road, an abandoned railroad bed, where strange illuminations occurred at night; it attracted many curious spectators, and not even the skeptical scientists had satisfactorily explained the phenomenon. Now Elizabeth Hall might become a character in local lore and conjecture, along with an Indian from the reservation and a tourist from New Orleans. What would the storytellers make of that? It was spooky to contemplate, and she shuddered in spite of Mark's assurances.

"We'll get out, Beth, I promise you. Meanwhile, we'll survive. There's food in here—we just have to find it. Might be rough for awhile, but nothing's going to happen to you. I won't let it."

"The way you didn't let losing us happen?" Ken scoffed. "Can you make a fire, Indian? Send smoke signals, or is that a lost form of communication?"

"Who'd see it unless from a helicopter? There's no wind to carry the smoke above the trees, and even then they'd think it was some crazy camper or poacher. Nobody knows we're in here, remember?" He cast about for the tallest tree, sighted a sycamore. "I'll climb up there and see if I can spot a house or road somewhere. People do live in the Thicket, you know."

Shucking his boots, he scaled the sycamore as easily as a lizard, gazed in every direction, descended dejectedly. "Nothing. Just Thicket, all around us, as far as I could see. And like you said earlier, Ken, it all looks alike."

"And you said you were marking the trail, mentally and instinctively. Where's your instinct now, Little Wolf?"

Beth intervened, "I'm hungry and thirsty."

"That pond looks stagnant," Ken said. "I suppose it's useless to ask if you have any purifier in your pack, like chlorine pills?"

"Useless."

"Oh, great. That means immediate canteen rations. How much have we got left?"

"About three halves, I'd say. But my canteen's an old metal one. We can boil baygall water in it."

"That'll help, if it doesn't melt. Now for food. Some cookies and raisins, the jerky, and whatever else we can scrounge. But no gun to shoot game, not even a bow and arrow. Some Indian!"

"I got a good bow at home."

"Fine, but we're here."

"I didn't expect to need it," Mark said defensively. "But we do have a weapon, anyway. A bowie knife."

"Know how to use it?"

"I think so."

"You could wrestle a deer or wild hog and slaughter it?"

"I could try."

"Hell, Mark. You'd end up dead, and we don't need that. No hatchet or collapsible shovel, either? Those are Boy Scout standbys in the field."

"Extra weight I'd have to tote, too. Besides, I'm not and never was a Boy Scout."

"Nor much of an Indian scout, either, unfortunately. So we'll have to gather wood. You do have matches?"

"Sure."

"Congratulations. I was afraid we might have to rub sticks together, since I lost my cigarette lighter somewhere in the brush. All that bending, twisting, crawling, to reach this goddamn impasse."

"God, I really blew this, didn't I?" Mark was morose and remorseful. "You got every right to ride me. I feel like killing myself."

"Nobody's perfect," Ken relented.

"But I wanted to show you up," Mark confessed. "A practical joke, you know? Got the idea when we were rapping at that other camp. Thought it'd be fun to scare you. Pretend to be lost, just to see your reaction. Then I'd bug you with tribal tales of Indian bravery and white cowardice. Grandpa used to entertain me that way, and the teenagers still play such tricks on the youngsters, inventing their own courage tests. I guess I concentrated too much on the game and not enough on the trail. The prank boomeranged."

"My fraternity brothers in college were always dreaming up stunts for the hazing rites," Ken reflected, "and some of them backfired, too. One pledge almost choked to death on a piece of raw liver forced down his throat, and another left tied in a fountain in February caught pneumonia and died."

Mark swallowed guiltily and reiterated, "We'll get out."

"How long do you think your mother will wait before looking for you?" Ken asked Beth.

"Probably until my midnight curfew."

"Meanwhile, she'll discover I'm also missing and possibly put one and one together. How about your family, Mark?"

"There's only my grandfather, and he's old. He'll think I spent the night with some friend in town, as I have before. But he won't come unglued. Indians his age don't get emotional. They say he was a radical firebrand in his youth, and a clever diplomat later. He went with the chief to Washington when the tribe was trying for recognition. Got some action too, if you could call a five thousand dollar appropriation action. Christ, how could the Treasury afford it! But he's eighty now, and just a benevolent old Uncle Tomtom. Not the kind of representative a tribe sends to the Congress of American Indians. Boy, I'd like to be a delegate to that convention, rip some things off my chest!"

His fire and zeal supplemented any decline in his grandfather's. But he was still a boy, and his torch was primarily the sexual glow for a girl—a little white doll whose family would strenuously object to even a chief's son playing with her. Beth's susceptibility was a potential bomb, however, eagerly awaiting detonation. Ken knew he'd have to keep them both under steady surveillance.

"All that's in the future, Mark, and our concern is the present. Does it get cold here at night?"

"Cool, and the dampness makes it seem cooler. But if you have to get lost in the Thicket, summer's the best time. Winter's a bitch, and it's often a rain forest in spring. We'll have to sleep on the ground. No bedrolls, only a blanket for Beth."

"We'll share it," Beth offered. "That's got to be the first rule of survival—share and share alike."

Talking and planning alleviated some tension and anxiety. And daylight was reassuring. Night was the terror of the Thicket. Encompassing darkness, weird sounds, eerie gaseous lights on the marshes, prowling animals, crawling creatures. Armed hunters stayed close to camp and dogs at night. And they were novices with only a bowie knife for protection, which Mark subsequently used to cut each of them a small piece of venison jerky for supper. Tough and sinewy, overcured by his grandfather, it tasted like salty rubber and produced aching jaws and severe thirst; still, it was delicious, something to chew and savor while gathering firewood.

By six o'clock, evening was already on the floor of the Thicket, and even a full moon would not bring much light. The brightest sun was barely able to penetrate the massive tangle, so that in the deepest recesses of the undergrowth the earth smelled musty as a tomb. Whippoorwills began their plaintive calls long before twilight. Bobwhites whistled shrilly in the brush, droves mourned, owls hooted. Now and then a brief primal silence prevailed; it was only a few seconds before animal noises resumed, but it was long enough to send ominous vibrations through the uninitiated.

"Gee," Beth murmured in awe, "it's getting creepy."

Mark's hand comforted hers. "It won't get much darker than this until sundown."

"Ever spend a night in here?" she asked him.

"Baby, I was born in the Thicket."

"On the reservation. I meant alone, in the woods."

"With hunting parties several times, and other boys, but never alone," he said.

Beth watched wistfully as the last crimson glow faded from the sky and merged into a misty purple, like water colors run together and bleeding at the edges. Almost immediately small animals began to emerge from the shadows to drink at the pond, as youngsters who must have water before bedtime. Opossums, armadillos, squirrels, otter, wild mink, skunks. At dusk a family of deer appeared—buck, doe, spotted fawn—but catching sight and scent of the aliens, streaked swiftly back to cover. Beth anticipated an animal parade all night, but Mark assured her the bonfire would discourage them.

"When do we make it?" she asked.

"Now," he answered.

CHAPTER SEVENTEEN

Darkness, and the wilderness hearth. They sat semicircle on the blanket, cross-legged as primitives in council, the men sharing a rationed cigarette to conserve their dwindling tobacco supply. Beth declined a proffered puff, as her throat was too dry and thirst too high.

Mark said, "In your historical novels, some of which are pitifully inaccurate, the western pioneer gets most credit for the campfire, and Zane Grey acted as if his cowboy characters invented it to sit around on cattle drives and shoot the bull. But the Indians were on this continent over twelve thousand years before Columbus discovered it. Theirs is the true American culture, and they were the original campfire makers."

Ken argued for the sake of conversation, "Well now, if you want to get technical about it, Mark, consider the European Neanderthal, knocking flints together in the Stone Age to roast prehistoric animals. I think the caveman invented the campfire."

"Really?" Beth mocked. "I thought lil ole Eve switching her bare tail in the Garden made the first sparks fly."

Mark grinned appreciatively. "I'll buy that. She put the glow on Adam, all right."

"Cool it, kids, and stop that paw communication. There'll be no monkeying around in my presence."

"Oh, boy! Just what every girl dreams about, being marooned with a medieval duenna," Beth complained petulantly. "You're not my chaperon, sir!"

"For tonight and the duration of this safari, I am, missy, and don't you forget it."

"I think he's jealous," Mark jeered. "Doesn't want us to have any fun because he can't."

"Well, he can't stay awake forever," Beth giggled. "He has to sleep sometime."

Ken realized they were teasing him, like mischievous youngsters ridiculing an elder to divert themselves, probably out of restlessness and apprehension of the night. "Try me," he challenged, playing the game. "I used to stand twenty-four-hour guard duty in boot camp."

Mark gave a derisive snort of laughter. "That was years ago, man, when you were young and strong. You're pretty mush-muscled now. I noticed your huffing and puffing on the trail, when we had to crawl through 'tight-eye.' Don't you jog, exercise? Just sit on your tail at a plush desk all day, raising your bread on the yeast of other folks' dough? Talk about parasites! The investment counselor has got to be the champion bloodsucker in the entire leech system. Ever had to pound corn on a rock to eat? I used to help grind the meal for our sofkey—that's a corn gruel, papoose pablum, Indian diet staple; and it doesn't come out of a box or can yet. No assembly lines or surplus problems on the reservation so far. Survival's the principal industry, and it's a community project."

"It had better be a common effort now, too," Ken told him. "I don't know what about me you resent so much, Mark, but I wish you'd forget it until this is over, at least. Then it's okay with me if we never meet again."

"Hey now!" Beth objected. "What kind of rapping is that? You'll meet again, Ken, if you expect to be part of my family, because Mark definitely will be."

"Don't count on it, Beth, for either of us." Ken held his wrist to the blaze to see the time. Nine o'clock, but it seemed and felt later. He was fairly exhausted.

"Getting tired, old man?" Mark taunted, bear-baiting. "Want to sack in?"

In the Thicket a lonesome coyote howled, lost from his pack, or a desperate bachelor despairing of a mate. "Careful, boy. I'm not that much out of condition or prime. I could beat your breechclout off any day in the moon calendar."

"Don't you mean jock strap? I'm an athlete, re-member? And if you'd like to test your physical prowess, put your arm where your mouth is and wrestle Indian style." Positioning his elbow eagerly on the blanket, "I'll take you in the grip, pronto. Beth can be referee."

"No, thanks. I'm sure you're an expert wrestler in many fields, Little Wolf. Just don't practice any clinches with Fair Maiden."

Their precipitous hostility worried Beth. There was some kind of chemical incompatibility between them, as explosive as nitroglycerin when disturbed —and she seemed to be a disturbing factor. She wanted to rap their knuckles with a stick and knock their stubborn skulls together. "Come on now, fellas, find some other amusement. Tell stories or make up lies—it's too early to turn in. Listen—isn't that a sweet little nightingale in the sycamore?

Maybe the darling will serenade us all night. Oh, what a beautiful sound!"

Ken smiled. "No offense, honey, but right now I'd rather hear a bulldozer and see a whole caravan of modern Ahabs in mechanical monsters plowing a path to us."

"You copout easy," Mark muttered.

"When it's Mother Nature versus man, Indian, the gentle old lady can be a perverse and perverted bitch. And she doesn't surrender easily, either. She fights back like a vixen and often wins. I bet this jungle contains the bones of many of her victims, including some of your ancestors."

"Many, but Indians were and still are born knowing they have to fight for survival. And most 'savage heathens' managed well enough until the 'Christian saviors' came to civilize them with Bibles and bayonets. Overpopulation was no problem, because they weren't such prolific breeders as other races and had a high infant mortality rate, particularly after the Caucasian communicated all his infectious diseases. But it was really warfare that ruined them."

Beth said timorously, "I'm not copping out, Mark, but I think I'd like to hear some civilized sounds too now. It's so dark and wild in here."

Mark motioned for the smoke. Ken relinquished the cigarette. Mark inhaled pensively, surrendered it again. Then his eyes sought Beth's in the firelight. "I gather you would not want to live in the Thicket?"

"You mean on the reservation?"

"I guess that's what I mean, yeah."

"I'm not sure I could, Mark. And why should we? Lots of Indians live off the reservation. Money wouldn't be a problem. I'll inherit a mint at twenty-one."

"That's five years away," he brooded.

"But I'll be eighteen in only two years. And I wouldn't want a fancy place, Mark. Just an apartment somewhere, alone and together."

Blowing smoke rings, Ken drawled, "Watch it, Beth. You're making unconscious commitments."

"Not unconscious," she said.

"Naïve, then."

"Not naïve, either."

"But maybe Mark wouldn't be happy any place else? Maybe all he wants is a tepee in the Thicket, with his and her bearskin rugs. And he knows life off the reservation would be difficult for both of you. You're only confusing him, because you're confused yourself. So why don't you just turn off this heavy stuff and onto something else? You know, this experience needn't be a total waste for any of us. It could be educational, a sort of cultural exchange seminar. Mark, tell me the history of your people."

"My people are the Coushattas—and they have no written language, no recorded history. It's all derived from legend, and it's too long to tell even if I thought you were really interested, which I don't. It's just another of your ploys to keep Beth and me apart. Permanently, you figure, if she can be convinced how difficult it would be for us to hack it together. White men have always tried to outwit Indians by reason or force—and trick or kill them when they couldn't succeed. Unfortunately they usually succeeded, which is why we're the vanishing race. But we've wised up some in the last century. We're not so easily conned any more."

"You're snarling again, Little Wolf. What are you, the reservation rebel or something? I reckon you won't be satisfied until we tangle tooth and claw. But I don't care to exert the energy now. So blow off your goddamn steam some other way. Dance with Pretty Maiden. Just keep moving."

The suggestion appealed to Beth, who was growing increasingly restless and fearful of unseen terrors. She longed for a diversion, particularly one that would put her and Mark in intimate contact. "Oh, would you, Mark? Please? Teach me a tribal dance?"

"Like the Na Ski La Dancers perform for tourists in their 'colorful buckskin and eagle feathers,' as the brochures say?" He frowned. "You know how I feel about that, Beth. It's a tribal enterprise, to make money to feed and clothe us. We're in show biz now, baby. We're actors, performers, hawkers, entrepreneurs. We're building a reptile garden and enlarging the restaurant to accommodate more visitors, and we're grateful for their business. It keeps us going. But as my grandfather says, sooner or later in a civilization based on currency, everything reflects gold and loses all other significance. The dance routines are memorized and practiced so often they're mechanical now. But they used to be symbolic. Each chant, every step and stamp were significant, and there were many variations. The New Fire Dance, for instance, was a busk religious ritual. Sacred."

"They worshiped fire?" Ken asked interestedly.

Mark was well enough versed in tribal history and lore to lecture in the reservation museum, which he sometimes did. Other times he demonstrated crafts, or drove a vehicle on the forest tours, or worked on the "Indian Chief" railroad, or in the restaurant featuring "authentic tribal food."

Now, resting his elbows on his knees, he gazed

191

into the leaping orange-red flames, as if mesmerized. "Fire was a mystery to them; they believed the Divine Spirit dwelt in it. All the natural forces were basic in their religion: the sun, moon, stars, rain, wind. Good elements were considered a blessing, bad ones a curse. Savage, superstitious? Maybe, but at least they revered supernatural things, not the idols and fetishes worshiped by your pagans and barbarians. They didn't practice any more witchcraft than some of your ancient cults and sects, either. Agreed?"

Ken nodded mutely, wishing he knew his own genetic history, of which he was and would likely remain totally ignorant. In the jungle dark.

"As for the fine art of cruelty and torture," Mark continued, "who invented the rack, and threw people to lions, and stuck heads on poles over bridges, and burned at the stake?"

"Indians burned at the stake too, man, and scalped, and tied live victims in red ant nests. They weren't all happy, carefree, painted clowns entertaining the wagon trains."

"Not all, no, any more than the white men were all missionaries and good scouts. The Comanches, Kiowas, Apaches raided, raped, and killed for the hell of it. And the Karankawas, in the Thicket when Spaniards first arrived, were bloody cannibals. No doubt there were renegades among the Coushatta, too. But most were peaceful. They made peace and friendship with solemn rites. But they weren't cowards and fought when necessary. Then the warriors prayed and fasted and drank purifying emetics before going into battle, in the hope that the Great Spirit would understand their cause and help them win honorable victory."

"Gee, all that was so heavy, Mark," Beth said,

admiring his profile and the coppery gleam of his flame-burnished skin. "I know they had celebrations just for fun and games, too."

"Sure, they were human—and they laughed and played and loved like other humans. They had planting and harvesting feasts. Social games and competitive sports. Births and weddings were always joyous occasions, with singing and dancing. Rawhide drums, gourd rattles, and cane flutes were the usual musical instruments."

"Groovy," Beth murmured.

"You've seen the Green Corn Dance. It's one of our favorite commercials and should be sponsored by some cereal company making Maize Toasties or something. Exploit our talents a little more and collect residuals. Why not? The white man taught the Indian the decimal dollar system. He had to learn to trade and barter, not only for goods but for his land and life. And up until the American Indian renaissance a few years ago, nobody gave a damn. The only good Indian, according to General George Custer, was a dead Indian. Now it's a sort of national conscience craze, like the black issue. But there're still plenty of whites who feel like Custer about both races."

"True, but who do you think is going to hear you howling in the wilderness, Little Wolf?"

"Maybe you, Tatka-Na-Ne."

"Tatka what?"

"Tatka-Na-Ne. Muskogean for paleface."

"I thought you were Coushatta?"

"Coushattas are Muskogean stock, and they've kept the language pure."

"The blood too, as far as possible, from what I've read," Ken said. "They don't believe in interracial marriage. Don't they prefer Coushatta women and

haven't they in fact taken squaws from the Louisiana tribe?"

Beth leaped to her feet, furious with him. "Damn
you, Kenneth Steele! What're you trying to do to
me? The only reason I arranged this trip was so
you could get to know Mark, and I thought you
were on our side. But you're bucking us all the
way. Why, for God's sake? You can't make brownie
points with Mom out here."

Mark's face split in a grin. "End of council." He
stood, stretching his panther-lean body toward the
star-spangled sky. "Now we hit the blanket."

"If there's any doubt about the sleeping arrangements," Ken said, "I'm in the middle."

Mark walked wordlessly away.

"Where're you going, Cochise?"

"Me go privy, Tatka-Na-Ne. Okay?"

"Shove the Tatka-Na-Ne."

"Shove the Cochise."

Beth said timidly, "I've got to go too, and I'm
scared of the dark."

"I'll hold up the blanket for you," Ken offered.

"Wow! Toilet training's gonna be a gas in the
morning, Daddy Dear."

"Hurry up," Ken ordered, erecting the woolen
barrier, "while Mark is occupied."

"Yes, sir."

When finally they were bedded down in the
designated positions, Beth murmured, "Now I lay
me down to sleep . . . say your prayers too, Mark."

"Oh, Ha-Ce-Ha-Pah! Let Indian be good. Let
Indian be well. Let Indian kill deer."

"Let Indian shut up," Ken muttered.

"You jerk! I was trying to teach you something.
That's the old tribal Lord's Prayer. Kids learn it at
their mother's knee. Our forefathers said it to the

new moon. When the missionaries came and convinced them that God made the moon, they said
it to God instead. Ha-Ce-Ha-Pah is Muskogean for
Great Spirit."

"I'm sorry," Ken apologized. "I thought you were
just clowning again, calling me hotsy-papa or some
such crazy name. I didn't know, Mark."

"There's a lot you don't know, man."

"I'm learning," Ken said. "And I hope we're all
in a better humor and more receptive mood tomorrow. This entire evening's performance has been
nine-tenths bravado for all of us, I think, rather like
whistling in the dark. Good night, kids. Bright
dreams."

Mark formed a finger V above their heads.
"Peace."

"Love," echoed Beth.

The lonely coyote had become a yodeling trouba-
dour. Soon a prowling bobcat began his armorous
serenade, spine-chilling. Then the shrill squeals of
two javelina boars in competition for a sow. Of all
the sexual calls, however, familiar to Mark since
childhood, the passionate bellows of the bull alli-
gators were the most welcome now, for they meant
a stream or bayou in the vicinity—fresh water and
possibly even an inhabited house on the banks. He
would hunt for it tomorrow.

"Jesus," Beth shuddered, "how could anyone
sleep with all that racket? They seem so close,
almost on us."

"Sound carries here," Mark explained. "Bounces
and echoes off trees. The acoustics are terrible."

Ken asked if the knife was handy.

Mark answered, "We won't need it. They're after
each other, not us. And the fire will keep their
distance."

"Just keep yours," Ken warned again.

But he didn't reckon with youthful determination. Walking around midnight he found them together on the other side of the fire, silhouettes of urgency. And he was furious, not at being outsmarted but disobeyed. He raged in his fury, "Mark, you sneaky coyote! Let her alone!"

"We're not doing anything," Beth protested. "Honest. Just kissing goodnight. Can't you see?"

"Get away from him, Beth, and button your shirt. If you pick up a papoose, it's not going to be on this expedition and my conscience!"

"You sonofabitch!" Mark said and lunged at him, knocking them both to the ground, battling as fiercely as any of his animal counterparts in the Thicket over the female of the species. "You goddamn bastard!"

Sprawling, thrashing, cursing, while Beth screamed and pulled at them. "Stop it, you crazy fools! Oh, go ahead, kill each other, and leave me here to die alone! Mark! Ken!" She knew fighting dogs could be separated by a dash of cold water and wished for a pail to dip from the baygall. Pleas failing, she grabbed a stick of burning wood and threatened to brand them. Finally, she threw herself desperately into the fracas, and it worked like magic; they would not hurt her, though they might rip each other to pieces.

Upright again, brushing himself, Ken muttered, "Next time I'll cream you, Little Wolf."

"It wasn't his fault, Ken. It was mine. I lured him."

"Oh, let him rave, Beth. It's been a contest from the beginning, and you're the prize. That's his problem, and he knows it. It's the old wilderness call—turns men into beasts, and the old beasts are the worst, selfish and greedy and aggressive. And jealous as hell of the young ones. Every autumn I watch the old bucks challenge the yearlings for the does. Sometimes they win, too. Most of the time, in fact, because the old bastards have more combat experience. And they're also more cunning, ruthless, desperate, and violent."

"You finished, Little Wolf?"

"Unless you'd like a rematch, Tatka-Na-Ne."

"I'd like some sleep," Ken said. "Shall we try again?"

CHAPTER EIGHTEEN

With the nightly drop in temperature Beth grew cold and in her sleep snuggled childlike to warmth. Ken wanted to comfort and protect her; this might be as close to fatherhood as he would ever come. But Mark's savage jealousy and earlier accusations, which he realized now were not entirely baseless, deterred him. The boy's instincts and perception were keener than his own, his objections justified. In all honesty, he was sensually stimulated by the girl's proximity, and his desire to turn and embrace her now was not entirely paternal.

The fire was burning low, almost to embers. He should rise and rekindle it. But he couldn't remove himself from her deliberately, nor disturb her enough to change positions and abandon him. He watched the smoldering coals and listened to the Thicket creatures. Commercial jets passed overhead, red and green lights blinking. Apparently they were in some kind of air traffic pattern, which would probably make small craft searching difficult and hazardous. Beth sighed and moved, cuddling herself into a kittenish ball, and his sense of loss and desertion were extreme, depleting, painful.

Dawn, finally. The gray shaft of morning de-

scending arrow-straight upon them. Ken had a fiend-
ish headache from lack of sleep and unalleviated
tension, and his heart was pounding in his ears.
No doubt his blood pressure had fluctuated during
the night. He scanned the brightening sky, hoping
to see or at least hear helicopters. But all he heard
were awakening Thicket noises, and all he saw was
a big black buzzard circling. drifting momentarily
out of sight, reappearing and hovering expectantly,
as if reconnoitering for a flock.

The kids woke hungry and refreshed. Beth was
clear-eyed and tousel-haired, with no fatigue
marring her smooth pretty face. Mark's bronze skin
unblemished except for a few battle-scars reflecting
the nocturnal confrontation: a bruised cheekbone,
and mouth abrasion. But he'd taken some blows
also and could feel a sore jaw and slightly puffed
lip. Also a sandpapery chin.

Beth yawned and stretched, orienting herself.
"Gee, it's really true, isn't it? We're lost in the
Thicket. I was hoping it was only a dream."

"Afraid not, honey," Ken said.

She loosened her braids and began to replait
them. "I'm starved. What's for breakfast?"

"A cookie and some water. We'll save the jerky
for supper, and forage for food near camp. Catch
frogs, dig crawdads by the pond, whatever is necessary. Some people eat ants and grasshoppers, you
know."

Beth grimaced. "Fried or chocolate-covered. I
don't think I could go for them raw."

Mark was up and flexing his muscles like a year-
ling deer. "We heard gators last night. That means
a creek or bayou in the vicinity, and a chance for
fresh water. I don't know how near or far, though.

Their roars are powerful and carry for miles. I'm not even sure of the direction, but I'll look."

Ken said, "Just don't get lost again."

"Don't worry," he replied sheepishly, "I'll stay in shouting range. Keep the fire burning, in case they're hunting us," and loped off, cookie in hand.

"What's that emblem he's wearing?" Ken asked Beth. "A tribal symbol?"

"Just Indian jewelry. Mark made it himself in the craft shop. But it's patterned after a Muskogean sabia—that was a charm supposed to bring good luck in love, war and hunting."

Ken smiled. "They equated the three activities?"

Beth ate her cookie slowly to make it last longer. "Well, I guess they have much in common, don't they? The sabia must have worked with women, anyway, because there used to be a lot of Indians around. Mark's making me a charm bracelet. He's very talented with his hands."

"Yeah, I noticed last night. Am I marked?"

"Just a few scratches. He drew blood, but so did you. I'd call the fight a draw—but I bet Mark would have won if it'd lasted longer."

"No doubt. The advantage of youth. It has many advantages, Beth."

"Really? Sometimes I wonder."

"Take my word for it. Young is better. Young is stronger. Young is more beautiful."

"Young is hungrier, too. And thirstier. God, I hope we can find something good to eat. Like nice plump juicy berries, or wild watermelons. There're all sorts of goodies in here, if you're lucky enough to find them."

Thicketeers knew where the best blackberries, dewberries and raspberries grew, as well as mustang grapes, wild plums, peaches, and pecans and other nuts. They knew which leaves and roots were nutritional and medicinal. The elders of the Indian village knew these things, too. But how much practical survival knowledge Mark had accumulated in his nineteen years remained to be seen, and Ken was an alien in this territory, while Beth was a virtual babe in the woods.

After an hour of foraging the camp periphery, they were still empty-handed. And periodically the water scout communicated his location and failure with a lusty yowl.

"Little Wolf's still with us," Ken said. "You answer him this time, Beth. My throat's getting hoarse."

Beth played a game, singing out, "Ten o'clock, and all's well!"

Ken discovered an edible plant. "This is pokeweed, Beth. Countryfolk eat it in Louisiana, especially Negroes."

"I know. Maple says the young shoots taste like asparagus. But it has to be cooked, Ken, and we don't have any kind of utensil. Remember where it is, though, in case we have to eat it raw and risk dysentery." She paused. "Did you know Maple was born in Louisiana? Her family lived in the swamps and came to Texas when she was ten. She said they used to eat possum and wild yams and pokeweed and all sorts of stuff. I love to hear about her childhood, but Grandma doesn't like for Maple to tell me about it."

"Why not?"

"Oh, she thinks I'll compare it to mine and feel guilty, and I do. It's strange, the way she and Mom look at things—or don't look at them. They both consider poverty and suffering and misfortune mere facts of life for some people. And race, too. Indians

201

are Indians, Mexicans are Mexicans, Negroes are Negroes. God made them that way, and He must have had a reason. They don't have anything against race or color, or in common with it, either. They'd do anything for Maple—nurse her when she's sick, lend her money when she's broke, help her out of a jam if she got into one. But she'd still be Our Maple, as if they owned her—Black Maple, Servant Maple, not Maple Borden, woman, friend, person. You know what I mean?"

"I think so," Ken nodded. "Never the twain shall meet. How do you feel about it?"

"Well, I think of her as Mrs. Martin Borden, mother of a son in college, wife of a paper mill worker. Members of the community, living in a neat little house, going to church, taking Sunday drives, having picnics and problems. People. Like I think of the Mexicans. And Indians."

"Especially one Indian? If you marry him, how will you sign your Christmas cards? Beth and Wolf?"

She wrinkled her pert nose at him. "Beth and Mark Carradine, that's how. I think it's a perfectly beautiful name, lyrical. I like yours, too. Steele sounds strong, permanent. Promise me something, Ken."

"What?"

"You'll marry Mom soon as we get out of here."

"I'm not at all sure she'll have me, Beth."

"Don't be ridic! She's as gone on you as I am on Mark. And I want you for my father, Ken. Do you want me for your daughter?"

"You know I do, honey. Hey, I think I see a mulberry tree! Maybe the crows haven't sacked it yet. Come on!"

It was a big tree, loaded with ripe fruit, for

which they had to fight their feathered friends, hurling rocks and sticks into the branches and stripping the lower reaches between barrages and bird retreats.

"Eureka!" cried Beth, cramming a fistful of berries into her mouth, swallowing some whole, black juice trickling down her chin, staining her skin darkly.

"Take it easy," Ken cautioned. "You'll get a tummyache." But he gulped handfuls, too. They watched each other, laughing, enjoying, and then Beth said, "Your chin is black. I bet mine is, too. But I don't care. I'd like to roll naked in mulberries and be black all over!"

Ken stopped laughing. "We'd better pick some for camp."

"Give me your shirt to put them in," she said. "I'd use mine, but I'm not wearing a bra." And as Ken obliged, she said, "Indians don't have hairy chests."

"You've seen Mark's chest?"

"Sure, and more."

"Don't tell me about it, Beth."

"Why'd you ask, then, if you didn't want to hear? You're curious, and you know it. Don't be a hypocrite."

She fashioned a basket from the garment, tying sleeves and tails together. Ken concentrated on filling it. Mark warbled another tremolo, and Ken said surily, "There's your Indian love call again. Answer."

"Yahoo! Yahoo!" It echoed off the trees melodically, and the mockers tried to imitate it.

"I think this is enough, Beth. We can find the source again. Let's go back."

In camp they stashed the reserve in the brown paper bag and suspended it from a branch with vine-string to discourage the ants, and then Ken donned his shirt again now darkly stained as if with India ink.

A jet liner flew over like a giant silver hawk trailing vaporous tails. "More commercial stuff." Beth despaired. "I haven't seen or heard a helicopter yet, have you?"

"No, but they surely know we're missing by now and are looking for us."

"Maybe, but not in the Thicket, Ken. Mom would have the Civil Air Patrol and squadron of company planes and choppers in the sky if she thought I was in here. Not to mention the Forest Rangers and a few sheriffs' posses."

"Well, she knew I wanted to see the Thicket, Beth. I told her so, and she ordered me not to mention my interest to you. But eventually she's bound to connect us."

Beth shrugged. "I'm always threatening to run away, Ken. She might think I finally split. Just saddled up my pony and rode west."

"She'll check the stables and find Brute there."

"So she'll know I'm not on horseback. That leaves the bus or thumb-tripping."

"I'll stroke the fire, anyway, and hope the smoke rises high enough to attract attention. A helicopter could rescue us by air, but more likely it'll take a search crew with dogs. They can get the scent from our clothes. And once they find the car and where we entered—"

"It seems so long already, Ken, like we've been gone for days, lost forever."

"That's because we're isolated and idle," Ken said. "Time always drags under those conditions. If we just had a deck of cards, or paper and pencil to write a log..."

"I'd settle for a bath, right now. I feel so sticky. No soap, toothpaste. We're going to stink like skunks. And in three more days, I'll have the curse. Maybe."

"What do you mean, maybe?"

"Oh, I'm either late or early, rarely punctual. Not regulated yet, Doc Ramsey says."

Ken gazed at her seriously. "Is that the only reason, Beth? It couldn't be anything else?"

"You mean Mark?"

He nodded. "You've been with him, haven't you?"

"Once," she admitted, "while Mom was in New Orleans. But he used a thing, got it from a rest-room vendor."

"Was it the first time?"

"For me, yes."

"The sonofabitch."

"Why? We love each other."

"But you're too young for that!"

"Too young for what? Sex? Not according to nature. And so I'm not a virgin any more. Is that some kind of tragedy? I'm glad it was Mark."

"Did he get to you again last night?"

"You know better."

"He tried, though."

"It was mutual. He's not an animal, Ken."

"He fights like one."

"You provoked him."

"Beth, listen to me. If you want to act like an adult, think like one. Surely you realize your family is not going to welcome Little Wolf to its bosom?"

Her gray eyes smoked with angry resentment. "You're meddling again, mister. I don't care about my family's bosom. I'll welcome him to mine."

Mark emerged from the Thicket before Ken could

say more. "Couldn't find the gators," he said. "They must be much farther away than they sounded."

"Ken and I found a mulberry tree," Beth announced happily. "We brought you some. Look in the bag hanging from the tree."

"Later, Beth. I'm not hungry now, just thirsty We'll have to boil some baygall water. Lucky there's no salt in it. We might have to use a dowser to locate more."

"Maybe it'll rain?" Beth said hopefully.

The sun was at its zenith, a brilliant fireball searing the bleached sky. "No chance, baby."

"Well, don't do any rain dances," Ken said. "They might be hunting us with hounds, and they lose smell in water, you know." No doubt some of his distant relatives could testify to that, having been scent-tracked in the swamps and jungles of the past. Coon hunts, the big white plantation hunters had called the pursuits of runaway slaves.

"We didn't walk in any water," Mark said, glaring at him malevolently. It was primarily to avoid the known marshes and bogs that he'd selected that particular route, in fact, and everything would have been fine if he'd just kept his mind on guiding. But he'd gotten uptight about Steele in relation to Beth, forgot his business, and fouled up completely. His grandfather, Wise Wolf, would call him a jackass. And his father, Big Wolf, must be rolling over in his burial mound.

"I know that, Indian, but the searchers won't."

"What searchers? They don't seem to be coming from above, guided by the Great White Spirit."

"I don't care if they come from below, led by the Great Black One," Ken said, "as long as they come."

CHAPTER NINETEEN

Mark was devising a gig for frog-hunting, securing the bowie knife to a long straight stick with vine-tendrils. Beth watched with salivating anticipation. After two days of a near-starvation diet, hunger pangs gnawed in her belly, and she was obsessed with a desire for substantial food. Roasted bullfrog legs, a delicacy in gourmet restaurants, tasted like breast of chicken. And tomorrow Mark could rig up some traps for quail or wild turkey if there were any about, although they hadn't heard any gobblers trumpeting in the woods, nor seen any prairie chickens.

"You see anything good to eat while you were scouting out there?" she asked Mark, moistening her dry lips with the tip of her slightly-swollen tongue.

"A wallow of wild hogs and a couple of deer."

"Wow, barbecued pork and venison! Couldn't you steal a shoat or coax a fawn to follow you to camp?"

"I thought of it, but they had some mean critters guarding the sty. Trying to catch pigs greased with bear fat used to be an old Indian sport, but they didn't fool much with javelinas; the boars can rip a man to ribbons. And even a track runner can't beat a deer in its country. I saw some mustang grapes but they're still green. And a pecan tree, but the squirrels and possums had already gathered the nuts, so maybe we can barbecue one of them."

Yesterday the thought of killing any of these creatures would have been abhorrent to Beth. So Ken was right, after all, self-preservation was the first and strongest instinct. Already they were reverting to primitives, bearing out all the wilderness legends, and she was too hungry to care. The Thicket had become their enemy, a powerful green giant, which they must challenge and conquer to survive. Man versus nature, just as Ken had said, and he was standing on the sidelines now, smoking and contemplating the battle.

"That looks like a serviceable spear," he told Mark. "Think you could make a bow and arrows?"

"I could try, I guess. Should be some good bow material around here, though ironwood trees are the best, and I don't see any. A resilient vine might do for the string, and I could whittle some quivers. Then, if a blind deer with no sense of smell or hearing got close enough, I might be able to hit it or scare it to death."

Ken laughed and offered the cigarette. "We've got seven smokes left—you didn't happen to see any wild tobacco?"

Mark inhaled. "Not even any hemp."

"The kind of pot we need most is one to cook in," Beth said, thinking of the pokeweed shoots. "Wonder if I could find a useable tincan in that trash pile?"

"If you do, it'll be a strainer," Mark predicted, "riddled with bullet holes. The hunter always use them for target practice."

Some splindly saplings, too much deprived of sun to ever mature, had sprouted around the dump, as if to camouflage it. Animals had been digging the lode, and before one of the burrows a diamond-back lay coiled and alert. Beth did not see it until she heard the warning rattle, then she screamed bloodily and froze in terror.

"Don't move," Mark cautioned in a whisper. "He'll strike at any movement. He's trying to hypnotize you. Keep quiet and stare back at him. I'll think of something—"

He signaled Ken to silence and immobility, too. Beth was petrified now, rooted to the spot, gazing stonily. The pit viper's head was elevated, tongue flicking and tail shaking menacingly, yet somewhat indolent and complacent with a refuse rodent in its belly, preferring to frighten and bluff rather than attack, hissing and puffing and rattling. Beth feared she might faint and topple onto it.

Mark planned to distract the snake by approaching from another angle, allowing Beth to retreat out of striking range. Moving stealthily around the midden, he held the spear poised, intending to throw it when close enough to connect. The diversionary tactic succeeded momentarily and Beth, thinking she was safe, stepped back. The motion recaptured the rattler's attention, it rose to strike, forcing Mark to act prematurely. He threw the lance, missed, and leaped in front of Beth, knocking her clear but catching the fangs himself, in his right leg, just above the knee. The victor slithered into the brush. The victim crumpled and cringed in pain.

"Oh, my God!" Beth cried, falling horrified beside him. "It got him, Ken! The goddamn thing got Mark!"

"I know, I saw it. But I couldn't do anything."

"The knife," Mark said. "Get it, Ken. Hurry—"

Ken retrieved the weapon, wrenched it apart, and slashed open the leg of Mark's jeans. "I've never done anything like this before, Mark. Tell me how—"

"I'll do it myself. Make a tourniquet."

Ripping a sleeve from his shirt, Ken fastened it around Mark's thigh. "Shouldn't we sterilize that blade in the fire?"

"No time," Mark said, operating on himself, cutting a cross in the wound, gritting his teeth. Blood spurted. Beth winced and averted her eyes. Mark suctioned the wound, spitting blood and venom, repeated the procedure, then fell back dizzily. "Can't any more. Somebody else, please . . ."

"I will," Ken volunteered.

"No, let me!" Beth pushed him aside. "I know how, Ken. I've seen first aid demonstrations at school."

She sucked the incision, expelling more blood and lymph and poison, which she knew could kill her if absorbed through broken tissue in mouth or throat. But she continued, retching once, nearly vomiting, until Mark bade her cease.

"That's enough, baby, and thanks. The rest is already in my blood. No way to remove it."

"I'll help you back to camp," Ken said. "Spread the blanket in the shade, Beth."

Mid-afternoon, and still no sight or sound of search craft. Mark needed a doctor; without serum he might die. His leg was already swelling, the knee thick and angry-red, the calf puffy. The needle-sharp fangs had penetrated deeply, leaving two evenly spaced scars. Oral suction could hardly have eliminated the full venomous injection, and only antitoxin could effectively combat it. Beth remembered what the instructor had told the class about untreated snakebite; how a strike in an artery or main vein could bring rapid death; how otherwise the rampant poison would saturate the body within three days, a crisis would follow, and the patient would either survive or perish.

Mark lay motionless to curtail circulation, sweat beading his brow, a faint flicker of constrained nerves about his mouth and rigidly controlled jaw. Beth knew he wouldn't grimace or complain, no matter the pain or discomfort; forbearance was a racial attribute. She had read that squaws remained stolid even in the agonies of childbirth. She wept internally for Mark. Such futile dignity, such wasted courage and nobility!

Ken asked, "Were you ever bitten by a rattler before, Mark?"

"Once, when I was ten, on the ankle. I was playing barefoot near our house. They had serum in the clinic."

"What did the Indians do before the clinic?"

"Cut off a finger or toe, if they got hit in a hand or foot. Every tribe had its maimed members. They also used clay and mud packs, herbs, roots—whatever the medicine man recommended. Then they kept a wailing vigil, and the person lived or went to the happy hunting ground."

Beth had to escape, temporarily, or burst into tears. "That's enough talking," she decided like a strict nurse. "Rest now, Mark. Try to sleep."

Moving out of his hearing, she worried, "His leg looks bad, Ken."

"He's young and tough, Beth, and the other bite may have given him some immunity. But why did this have to happen on top of everything else!"

Eyes misting, mouth quivering, "He did it for

me, Ken. He didn't care about himself, only me. He saved my life."

"You'd better eat something," Ken told her. "A cookie and some berries. And drink some water."

"I couldn't. My stomach hurts, and I feel blah."

"Nerves and excitement. Try to relax, Beth. All we can do now is wait."

"For what? They're not looking for us, Ken. No one is coming. We're going to die here, and I don't much care any more. I wouldn't want to live without Mark, anyway." She sat down forlornly.

Squatting beside her, Ken said, "That's nonsense, Beth."

"It's not! I love him, and he loves me. Hasn't he proved it?" She waited, gazing into the shadowy woods. "But Mom would never let me marry him with her blessing. So if he lives and we get out of here alive, we'll have to wait until I'm of age and run away together. Mom wouldn't have an Indian son-in-law and half-breed grandchildren if she could prevent it. She'd as soon have Negroes in the family."

Ken hesitated, weighing his knowledge, aware that he'd never have a better opportunity to impart it. "Then she'll never marry me, Beth, because that's what I am."

Her head swiveled. "Indian?"

"Negro."

"Oh, come on now, Ken! That's not funny."

"Am I laughing? I'm perfectly serious, Beth. I'm a quadroom, one quarter Negro. In this part of the country that means I'm Negro, legally and socially."

"But that's fantastic!"

"Why? Because I don't look it? That doesn't matter. Racially I'm black, descended of slaves. I didn't know it when I met your mother, however. I learned it only a few days ago."

"You mean you discovered it on that dumb ancestor hunt that brought you to Texas?"

"More or less," he nodded. "Actually, I think I'd suspected it for a year or so, after I found an old journal in my aunt's trunk. Some pages were torn out and some names of people and places obliterated. The information didn't jibe with what little my parents had told me of the family, and I wondered why my aunt should have the journal in her possession and why parts of it were missing or destroyed. Apparently it was some kind of plantation record, and the name on the cover was Steele. I asked if my great-grandfather had been an overseer. Aunt Selma couldn't—or wouldn't—tell me much of anything. Once she said she'd simply found the diary among her parents' effects and kept it because she considered it a rare manuscript of the era. When she grew mysterious and secretive about it, I decided to do a little background digging on my own. That's what I was doing in Woodland Cemetery the day I met your mother. Looking for tombstones that never existed, that couldn't possibly exist in a Southern cemetery at a time when even the churchyards separated dead souls. And they're still segregated in Woodland, I noticed."

Beth nodded. "We're only beginning to integrate the schools and public places now. But how did you find out all this stuff about your family?"

"Aunt Selma suffered a belated spasm of conscience or something," he said ruefully, "and wrote me the details in a long letter. My ancestors came to Texas during the Civil War, but not as pioneers to settle new frontiers. They were runaway slaves, fugitives with a price on their heads. They hid out in your forests and were helped by some Indians until the war was over. I don't know the tribe, but evidently they knew what it meant to be pursued. Ironic, huh? Maybe I can return the favor by helping an Indian now.

"Anyway, the news sent me into orbit for awhile. It was a helluva shock, like dying and being born again as another person—and one I'd never particularly wanted to be. Who wants to be black, except maybe in Africa? I think I went a little nuts, discovering that even my surname didn't belong to me but was appropriated from my great-grandparents' former master! I was planning to go excavating in the ruins of Bolden Plantation, where they eventually found work, when you called about the Thicket."

"You couldn't find anything at Bolden," Beth murmured. "I've seen it. Nothing left but some foundation posts and pillars and chimney rubble. Fire destroyed the whole bloody works long ago, and they say the ghosts of two slaves beaten to death there still haunt the place. But the forest has taken over the land again, thank God."

Ken picked up a twig, broke it in pieces. "Well, that's where my ancestral bones probably lie, Beth. In the 'nigger patch' at Bolden Plantation. And you know that old saw, Would you want your daughter to marry one? In this case, Would you want your mother to marry one?"

With a twisted stick Beth was drawing undecipherable hieroglyphics in the dust at their feet. "I'm not sure I can answer that honestly, Ken, because I don't see or think of you as black. But knowing it hasn't changed how I feel about you, so why should I object? I mean, if you love each other? You know that movie, 'Guess Who's Coming to Dinner'? All that heavy agonizing by the families—so dramatic and hokey. The only thing that was important, that made any real sense was how the two people concerned felt about it and each other. The way I see it, anyway. But Mom—well, white is the only way she'll have you, Ken. I could almost guarantee that. So if you want her, really want her, I wouldn't advise telling her the truth. I never will, I promise you."

"Darling girl." Ken took her hand, squeezing it harder than he intended, numbing her fingers so that she dropped the stick. "What about the hypocrisy your generation accuses mine of, the dishonesty and deceit?"

"This is different!"

"Only because you're personally involved, Beth. Would you lie about Mark's heritage?"

"No, not even if he wasn't so obviously Indian. But I'm not like my mother."

"Don't you think I know that, Beth? And don't you realize it's the reason why I couldn't possibly marry her under false colors?"

"But it's the only way," she insisted, close to tears. "I don't want to lose you, Ken, not after all we've been through together! I need you in so many ways. We both need you, Mark and me."

"Poor Little Wolf," Ken said, glancing at the stricken Indian, supine on the blanket, eyes closed, face still cast in its noble mold. "What was that Muskogean word for paleface? Tatka-Na-Ne? I wonder what they called black men?"

"Who cares?" Beth retrieved her hand. "Who cares about anything now? You know something? I almost hope we don't get out of here, because there's nothing for any of us out there now. Not any more."

Ken wanted to clasp her in his arms, soothe her agitated body, kiss her quivering mouth. "You don't mean that, Beth, and you surely can't believe it. You're young, a child. You'll live through this and eventually forget it and have a whole new life. And you'll be happy."

"How can you say that? I thought you knew me so well, but you don't know me at all. You think I'm still a little kid, and all this is just a bad dream. I'll wake to a bright new tomorrow and live happily ever after in a charming fairytale!" She scrambled to her feet, angry with him, hurt and disappointed that after all she'd confided he could still believe her so shallow and juvenile. "I'm going to Mark. You'd better boil some more water, in case he runs a fever. Mark needs me. You don't need me, Ken, or anyone else, apparently. And you don't really want me for your daughter."

"That's not true, Beth."

"Then why would you do something to deliberately lose me? Because you will, you know. But you'll still have your pride or honor or integrity or whatever the hell you want to call it that's making you such a stubborn fool about this. Well, I hope it's good company in your old age, Mr. Steele!"

Darling, darling, Ken thought, thinking of the child, not the mother.

CHAPTER TWENTY

Her helplessness frustrated, frightened, and infuriated Beth. Mark was going to die, she knew it intuitively, and there was nothing she could do to prevent it. She couldn't even attract attention by setting the Thicket afire, because they might all be trapped and cremated.

She kept a close vigil. Before sundown Mark was running a temperature, and she longed for a pail of cool water to sponge him. She'd have to use Mark's shirt, since Ken's had made the tourniquet and bandages. Removing the faded blue denim gently, she held it up to Ken. "Please dip this in the baygall."

He did and brought it back and Beth applied it to Mark's chest and arms. He was still conscious enough to smile his appreciation. Heartened, she tried to infuse vitality with a resuscitative kiss, but his vague, instinctive response only confirmed his weakness.

"If that doesn't help," Ken said, "nothing will."

He couldn't suppress his envy, nor delude himself any longer about its reason. Mark's suspicions and accusations last night had been justified, and his contempt and belligerence as well. Possessiveness,

217

not protection, had triggered the battle, and all other issues were superficial. He had represented the Indian's arch enemy, trying to steal something he valued, and he had attacked with traditional savagery. Ken couldn't blame him, either. She was a prize, all right; a treasure to be cherished and warred over. Beside the daughter, the mother was a pallid imitation of a woman, lacking substance, incapable of firm commitment. Their affair had released some pent-up sexuality in her loins and lust in his, which both had misinterpreted as love.

Beth gnawed her lip anxiously. "He's getting worse, Ken. His pulse is weaker, and hear how he breathes? That's a bad sign. And soon it'll be evening and dark again."

"At least it'll be cooler."

"But his fever is rising! Just feel this shirt—it's hot already. Dip it again, please."

Ken obliged, and she made another wet poultice. Despite her ministrations, however, Mark seemed to sink with the sun. He no longer reacted to touch or stimulation, but lay with closed eyes, breathing hard through his mouth, as if respiration were a labor. Beth put her ear to his chest; his heart had lost its steady drumbeat rhythm, sounding more now like an echo in a distant canyon. She held her fingers on his wrist.

"Florence Nightingale in the Thicket," Ken said.

"Robinson Crusoe," she replied, indicating his half-naked figure and stubbled face.

"Too bad there's no Doctor Livingston around."

"Do you believe in miracles, Ken?"

"No, I've never seen a miracle."

"Me, either. But Mark's not afraid to die, I know that. Indians don't fear death. And I don't fear it any more, either, for the reasons I told you earlier."

"Your father would be proud of you."

Beth brushed a persistent fly from Mark's face. "I doubt that," she said. "He'd probably want to kill both of you for getting me into this predicament and discount my own willful involvement. This isn't the kind of action Daddy used to praise at Chamber of Commerce and Rotary Club meetings. And it definitely isn't the kind Mom and Grandma admire."

Suddenly, over the treetops, the flapping of wings. A buzzard appeared and perched proprietarily in the dead cypress, black against the fading red sky. A companion promptly followed. Soon a small flock assembled in the gaunt branches.

"They know," Beth murmured. "They can smell death even before it occurs. I learned that in biology."

Ken scattered the creatures with a rock.

"They'll be back," Beth predicted glumly. "They know; you can't fool them."

"How did you accumulate as much knowledge in sixteen years, Beth?"

"Mark taught me much about the wilderness, while we were roaming the woods. You see, we didn't spend all our time making out. I wish now we'd spent more that way, though. More time together, too. I was hoping Mom would stay in New Orleans longer, maybe even forever."

Ken hunkered down beside her. "I proposed marriage to her there, Beth. She didn't want a hasty ceremony. Maybe it's a good thing. In retrospect, it all seems prophetic."

"Because of your blood? You're really going to use that excuse then, to let yourself lose her? Cop-out on race rather than fight for someone you love and want? You're a coward, Kenneth Steele, and

I'm ashamed of you. I don't know how I could have admired you so much this morning and be so disappointed in you now."

"You don't understand, Beth."

"Stop telling me that! I'm not a moron. I understand well enough, and a lot better than you might think. You don't love Mom enough to make the effort, and that's the plain and simple truth of it. If you did, nothing could stop you!"

"She doesn't love me enough, Beth, to commit herself all the way under normal circumstances, much less abnormal ones. She's been evasive from the start. And if she wouldn't accept an Indian son-in-law and half-breed papooses for grandchildren, what makes you think she'd want a Negro husband and octoroon pickannies of her own? And don't suggest secrecy and concealment again, because I'm not buying marriage on those terms, with your mother or anyone else. I've already struck out twice in that game; I'm not anxious for a third failure, which is all any union based on such a foundation could possibly be."

"Okay, we won't rap on it any more now." Beth conceded. "That's your stand, and you're entitled to it. I have a right to disagree, but it's your decision." Rising from the blanket, she said practically, "We'd better gather more wood to make sure there's enough for tonight."

They concentrated on that task and no other until they had sufficient fuel, careful where they stepped and what they picked up.

"We didn't even kill that monster," Ken regretted. "He got away and is still around."

"Mark tried—but did you know that primitive Indians never killed snakes? They believed the reptile's character would inhabit their bodies and take over their spirits after death. Their idea of reincarnation."

"Some African tribes still believe that," Ken said ruefully, "probably mine among them. I wonder where in the jungle my great-grandfather was born, delivered by a witch doctor, and in what abysmal ignorance and superstition he lived." He kicked fiercely at the woodpile. "Sorry, honey. Don't let me get maudlin on you. I guess it's time for chow, isn't it?"

A cookie each, a few raisins and mulberries, while the bullfrogs they had expected to eat still croaked and hopped in and out of the baygall. And there was no hope of barbecued pork or venison, either, now their hunter had slipped into a dense stupor.

"It's strange," Beth said, feeling almost satiated, "I was so hungry and thirsty before, and now the thought of food is repulsive. My stomach is actually cramping. I hope it's not the curse, on time for once." She wondered suddenly how primitive women coped with that problem; in all her reading she'd never come across the answer. Invented and improvised, no doubt. And while pondering her eyes fell on their primitive weapon, its blade still caked with the Indian's sun-dried blood. "For God's sake, clean that knife, Ken! Wash it in the pond . . ."

Evening brought a profusion of stars in the indigo sky but no brilliance from the crescent moon. Together they dragged the blanket and patient closer to the fire for protection against the night prowlers and crawlers. Mark rallied slightly when Beth forced some water down his throat, nearly strangling him so that he coughed reflexly and opened his eyes briefly. Then she refreshed his face and body with the damp shirt again and massaged his inert limbs. A sudden hard chill claimed him, and she warmed him with her person. His skin raging with fever burned hers on contact, but there was no sensory awareness in him. When his shivers ceased, she released him to oblivion again. This time Mark was in the center, and Beth lay beside him contemplating infinity. The vultures had returned at sundown to roost complacently in the cypress skeleton, an eerie scene against the tipped-canoe moon.

Nineteen, she thought. He'd hardly begun to live and already he was dying. And it was her fault. This whole stupid thing had been her crazy inspiration. She'd coaxed Mark and goaded Ken into it and insisted on their cooperation, conspiracy, and silence. Oh, she was a great one for secrets! Secret dreams, hopes, desires. Secret rides to secret places, secret meetings with Mark and secret love-making. Now they were secretly lost, and he was secretly dying, and she was secretly praying. Oh, Ha-Ce-Ha-Pah! Let Indian live. Please let Indian live.

Ken said, "That's the North Star up there, and ancient mariners navigated by it before the compass and sextant. They crossed thousands of miles of water guided by a star. And in a day when scientists are accurately charting astronomical flights, we're lost perhaps twenty or thirty miles from civilization. It's incredible! Even without a compass, we should have at least tried to get out."

"Mark thought it best to stay put." That was what they taught you to do in the Girl Scouts and Campfire Girls, too. Wait, not wander, if you got lost in the wilderness. "Don't you think it was the right thing to do?"

"According to the survival manuals, I guess. But

he'll probably be dead by morning, and what'll we do with him, then?"

Beth swallowed a lump in her throat. "Bury him."

"How? No shovel or pick, what'll we dig with?"

"Sticks. Hands. His tribe doesn't cremate by funeral pyre. There's a cemetery on the reservation, and his parents are buried there. I certainly won't let those filthy varmints up in that tree have him!"

"Darling, of course not. I shouldn't have said that, it was cruel. We'll manage somehow, do whatever we must." He longed to reach across the median, grasp her hand reassuringly. Instead he folded his arms beneath his head and watched the summer lightning, like a defective neon sign intermittently flashing. Static electricity, culminating an intensely hot day but rarely producing thunder or rain.

Night life was rousing in the Thicket, the familiar sounds amplified in the camp silence.

"Promise me something, Ken."

"What?"

"If I go before you, bury me beside Mark."

"Oh, Beth! Nobody is dead yet."

"Promise me?"

"Yes, yes, all right. And the buzzards get whoever's left, I suppose. But we're going to beat this, Beth. It's a bummer, but we're going to whip it."

"Sure. But just in case we don't, we might as well be prepared, don't you think? Do you have a will, Ken?"

"Yes. Aunt Selma is the beneficiary."

"Mom will get my share of the estate. But that's okay, because money is important to her. Almost as important as position. Sometimes she tries to pretend otherwise, but deep down she's just like Grandma."

"I know, honey. Know it only too well."

"I thought maybe you could change her, Ken."

"Afraid not," Ken said. "I'm not even sure I'd want to try any more now. One thing I do know, though. You've got more guts than anyone I've ever met, Beth. This is a nightmare for me, and by ordinary expectations you should be hysterical. Whoever said your generation was soft should have met you and Mark. I only hope somebody lives to tell this heroic tale."

A cloud obscured the crescent of the moon with a misty veil, and Beth said quietly, "That's a busk moon. The Muskogeans celebrated it with the Boskita—the religious ceremony Mark mentioned last night; fasting and dancing and purifying themselves before the harvest. And the Milky Way—they believed that was the Spirit Road which souls traveled on their journey to the happy hunting ground. They buried their dead sitting up and facing the sunset, so they'd be headed in the right direction, and gave them gifts and provisions. An old man got his pipe and tobacco to comfort him. Warriors and hunters had their bows and arrows, tomahawks and war-clubs, and some red paint for their faces. A woman would have her blanket and maybe some bright feathers and beads, to look pretty when she arrived in the Soul World. A baby was sealed in a hollow tree, to protect the tribe from spirits evil enough to take a little child."

"Did Mark inspire you to do all that research?"

"Some, but I've been hooked on Indians since my first trip to the reservation when I was seven. I have many books on Indian lore and history, and I'm collecting Indian art and artifacts. I get terrific grades on my Indian themes, and I'll probably write my college thesis on the subject. If I go to college."

"Certainly you'll go to college," Ken told her, as a firm father assuring a dubious child.

Mark stirred and moaned and sank deeper into the valley of the shadow. Coyotes bayed plaintively. The buzzards flapped and cawed. An unseen owl hooted. But the friendly nightingale was not entertaining tonight, and Beth missed it. Had it flown away? Had a hawk captured and killed it?

"Wonder what happened to Englebert?"

"Who?"

"Our singer."

"Oh. It's still early. He might sing later."

"Mark's so terribly still, Ken. In a coma, I think."

"It's better than suffering, Beth. What did the medicine men do for fevers?"

"Sweated the patient, in a hide-hut with hot rocks in vessels of steaming water. And gave them tea made from mulberry leaves to drink. Why didn't I think of that before? Tomorrow we'll get some leaves from that mulberry and boil them in the canteen. That might help."

"If he's still alive," Ken said.

"There're some natural antidotes to snake poison, but the medicine men who knew them kept them secret. Their knowledge was their magic, and they were jealous of it."

"Like the witch doctors," Ken said. "Beth, we'd better try to get some sleep. God knows what tomorrow will bring."

Beth sighed poignantly. "Sleep, with those vultures waiting? And Mark's wound is still seeping, Ken. Suppose a coyote or bobcat or javelina gets the scent?"

"The fire will discourage them. That big stump will burn all night."

The sky flashed repeatedly, like a luminous sheet fluttering, flaring, fading, flickering.

"It might rain," Beth worried.

"No, that's just heat lightning. Anyway, a shower wouldn't hurt any of us too much, would it?"

Beth laughed, surprised that she could. "Might be a godsend, in fact. I'm about ready to risk the baygall, cottonmouth moccasins and all."

"Me, too. Now close your eyes and try to sleep, baby."

The convulsions started in the damp predawn chill and continued unabated until the final spasm at sunrise. Beth had never seen anyone in the throes of death before, and its violence shocked and horrified her. The writhing, jerking nerves and muscles, the strange, harsh, rattlelike breathing. A hideous climax to life, and she'd never forget it. However long she lived, the memory would haunt her. Why did it have to end like this? Why couldn't he have gone peacefully in sleep? Yet she knew it would have been infinitely worse to wake and find him dead beside her.

She helped Ken hold Mark down on the blanket, lest he twist and roll into the fire, and when at last the horror was over, she had to be pulled away. There were no miracles. She cried in Ken's arms and he held her silently, and then wrapped the Indian in his blanket.

"You still want to bury him here, Beth? We may be able to get him to the reservation today? They're looking for us now, I think. Listen. Do you hear a helicopter?"

She nodded, trancelike. "A little late for Mark, though. We can't wait, Ken. Not in this heat, and with those damn monsters in that tree! We might as well start digging."

"I'll put more wood on the fire first," Ken said. "Once they spot the camp, they can airlift us out. Such rescues are made every day in Viet Nam. I think we're going to make it, Beth. Going to survive."

"For what, I wonder? What's in it for either of us now? It's a bigger thicket out there than in here, Ken."

"Sure it's rough, Beth, and it'll get rougher. But Mark gave his life for you, and I'm sure he had no regrets. The least you can do is not make his sacrifice in vain."

"If you'd left us alone the other night, I could have given him some happiness. And there wouldn't have been any regrets for me, either—no papoose like you feared, if that's the reason you fought with him. I—I know now why I was having those cramps, and it's not diarrhea." She would have to devise something from Mark's shirt.

"Well, you should be relieved," Ken told her. "Surely you didn't want to be pregnant?"

"I wouldn't have minded."

"Oh, my God, Beth! You've been sensible so far, don't blow it all now."

"Don't worry, Ken, I won't get hysterical. I'm not the type. Once, when I was twelve, my horse threw me in a pasture, and I was too badly hurt to remount immediately. I stayed there alone all day and came home at sundown hoping Mother wouldn't notice my injuries and torn clothes, because she'd warned me not to ride bareback and I'd disobeyed her. She warned me never to go into the Thicket too, and this time I really paid for my disobedience."

"It was fate, Beth. Mark would tell you that if he could. Indians are fatalists, aren't they?"

"Yes."

Ken was surveying the area for a likely grave site. It should be in the shade, and the soil under trees, combined with leafmold, was more friable and easier to work. "What about here?" he asked in the realm for the sycamore that Mark had earlier climbed for reconnaissance. Jesus, was it only two days ago?

"It looks okay," Beth agreed.

"I can manage alone, honey. You rest."

"No, I want to help."

"All right." Apparently it was something she had to do; so many of her actions seemed compulsive.

Somehow, with knife and sticks and hands and sweat and yielding earth, they excavated a ditch, shallow but accommodating. Together they placed the blanketed corpse in it and solemnly covered it.

"Do you know any tribal burial rites, Beth?"

"The Lord's Prayer will do," she said, suppressing tears. "After all, Mark Carradine was a Christian."

They prayed in unison, and then Ken constructed a cross by tying two sticks together with vine, while Beth piled a small pyramid of rocks Indian-fashion on the mound to discourage burrowing and scavenging animals.

When finally they retired to the shade of another tree, Ken said admiringly, "I want to tell you something, Beth—something I don't think I could say under any other circumstances. I envy Mark. Even dead, he's luckier than some live men."

"Oh, Ken!" She shook her head and bit her lip.

"It's true, and I mean it. He had you, however briefly, and nothing better could ever have happened to him, no matter how long he'd lived. He knew it, too. That's why he attacked me so violently the other night. He considered me a threat of some kind. That rattler also represented a threat. He was so afraid of losing you any way at all, he lunged at that snake as automatically as he did me. And he'd have reacted the same way to a wolf, panther, bear, anything to protect you." He paused wryly. "That's my eulogy to Mark Carradine, and all I'm going to say now."

A helicopter came into view directly overhead, hovering. Ken leaped up. "They've spotted us!" He shouted and waved his arms and then threw leaves on the fire to increase the smoke. "Come on out here, Beth, where they can see you!"

The helicopter disappeared, then reappeared with a couple of companions. Ken grabbed Beth and kissed her and swung her off her feet. "They see us! We're saved! We made it, baby! Thank God, we made it!"

The vultures, vacating their post, knew it too.

CHAPTER TWENTY-ONE

"Man, are we glad to see you!" Ken greeted the
first rescuer on the scene. "I'm Kenneth Steele, and
this is Elizabeth Hall."

"Don Harper," he said, extending his hand.

"Savior," Beth beamed.

"How long have you been hunting us?" from
Ken.

"Since late yesterday afternoon, when your car
was spotted. Had to stop at dark. There's a sheriff's
posse and dogs in the Thicket now. Hey, what's
that under the tree? Fresh grave?"

Ken nodded and explained.

Harper's expression mingled pity and surprise.
"We didn't know you had an Indian along."

"Our guide," Ken said without cynicism.

"Yeah, well it can happen in here—getting lost
—even with the best of 'em." He relayed the information electronically to the Ranger helicopter,
one of three involved in the mission, and awaited
instructions. "Roger. The girl up first. You want to
come over here, Miss Hall, and let me fasten you
in this rig."

Beth did not move, inquiring first if they would
also take the body of Mark Carradine.

"Afraid not, Miss. The sheriff will have to make that decision. This is his legal territory, you understand. He should arrive here before sundown."

"But I don't want to leave without him!" Beth cried. "You must have a net up there and room in one of the copters? He's already wrapped in a blanket, and we—we buried him only a few hours ago."

"I'm sorry, Miss Hall. I would if I could, believe me. But I have orders. Legal procedure."

"It's all right," Beth bribed, employing the Hall influence for one of the few times in her life, "my mother will square it with the law."

"In that case, they'll return for him," Harper reasoned. "Let's just get you and Mr. Steele airborne now, okay?"

"No, no! I told you, I won't go without Mark Carradine!" She ran to the grave and defiantly positioned herself under the sycamore.

Ken pursued her. "Beth, you're holding up the rescue. Come on now, be sensible. There's nothing more we can do for Mark—and what he wanted most was for you to get out of here alive." He took her hand persuasively; she yanked it away. "Baby, I'll knock you out if I have to."

"Go ahead, then," she challenged, firming her jaw, "because you'll have to, Ken. I'm not leaving without Mark! How could I after . . . after what he did for me?"

"Darling, for God's sake." Ken motioned to Harper, and together they managed to subdue her enough to secure her in the lift and send her aloft crying and protesting all the way.

"What a girl," Harper remarked admiringly.

"You don't know the half of it."

The seat descended again. Ken boarded. A signal from the ground coordinator elevated him. Once the operation began, it was completed swiftly and efficiently, as if it'd been performed many times before. Within an hour the survivors were landed at Woodland Airport, a small field and building now vibrating with beehive activity. Doctors, ambulances, police, press. And Mrs. Brian Tyson Hall aloof from the pandemonium, in the solicitous company and protection of her medical and legal aids and advisors.

Lanie welcomed her daughter with emotional tears, hugs, and kisses, while virtually ignoring her lover. Ken wondered what, if anything, the reporters had been told of their personal relationship. Probably nothing other than that he was a visiting friend. Cameras flashed and rolled, recorders taped, microphones were thrust into their faces. All hideously reminiscent of the aftermath of another tragedy.

"What happened in the Thicket, Mr. Steele?"

"We were lost."

"We know that, sir, but what happened?"

"Later, you guys," growled a bulldog of a deputy. "These folks gotta get to the hospital."

The newsmen danced attendance to the ambulance, and then encircled the vehicle preventing its escape.

"Did you know that Indian before the Thicket, Miss Hall? Was he a friend?"

"Let her alone!" Lanie said sharply. "Can't you see she's ill?"

"Did you ever give up hope of being rescued, Mr. Steele?"

Ken merely shook his head.

"How about you, Miss Hall? Any doubts of being saved?"

Beth nodded mutely.

"You and your daughter plan to attend the Indian's funeral, Mrs. Hall, if they remove the body to the reservation?"

Mercifully the deputy muscled in and shut the ambulance door, and they were off with wailing siren and police escort to Woodland Hospital. Immediately the survivors were examined, fed liquid nourishment, placed under observation. After several hours, during which Lanie patiently waited, they were pronounced in good condition and released.

It was evening then and almost dark, but the press camped on the porch and lawn of Whitney House, as tenaciously as the buzzards had kept their vigil in the Thicket. Lanie wished she had employed evasive action and gone to the estate instead, although an expectant flock was probably there, too. Hadn't they kept a long vigil during the search for the missing plane? Adventurers lost in the Big Thicket always made local news; when a VIP was involved it was a national story drawing the syndicates.

"Those calloused monsters," Lanie muttered. "Why can't they leave us alone?"

Ken rationalized, "We'll have to talk to them sometime, Lanie."

"Maybe you will, Ken, but not Beth or I. Just be careful what you say. I'd hate to have to qualify or deny any of your statements. As far as I'm concerned, this is all your fault!"

The legal battery, following in a tanklike sedan directly behind, arrived simultaneously and effectively escorted Mrs. Hall and her daughter into the house. Ken remained outside awhile, aware that the press corps had a job to do, supplying impersonal information, placating with promises of later interviews, finally retreating with an excuse that he was beat, only to confront Lanie in the library after Beth had been put to bed on doctor's orders.

The stately room, formal furniture, heavy draperies, leather-bound volumes—formidable as the judicial chamber in which the inquest into Michele's death had been held, and Ken felt as if he were about to undergo another one.

Lanie's joy and relief at having her daughter back alive in no way mitigated her fury at Ken for having risked her life in the first place. She would not absolve his guilt, nor forgive his irresponsibility any easier than had the Danielles what they considered his negligence. But at least he was spared Mrs. Whitney's wrath, for she had shut herself up in her room and remained incommunicado.

Shaggy haired, black beard bristling, pants dirty, torn and blood-stained, Ken looked like a derelict drifter. But someone at the hospital had thoughtfully provided a shirt for him, which fit fairly well. And unable to endure Lanie's accusing silence any longer, he said quietly, "All right, let's have it."

"Just like that, let's have it? As if you'd committed some slight social error that irritated me. Well, this isn't quite that simple, Ken, and I hardly know how to begin remonstrating. Have you any conception whatever of the hell you've put me through? I haven't been so worried and frantic since the long search for Brian's plane. When I realized you and Beth were together—well, I could have killed you, and I mean that literally! You knew how I felt about the Thicket, I told you in no uncertain terms. and yet you ignored my wishes and deliberately defied me."

"Lanie, it's over now. Beth is home, safe. A tragic

experience, yes, and I regret it desperately. But she survived it gloriously. She was terrific throughout the whole ordeal. I've never known anyone quite like her. I can't find adequate words to express my admiration. I'd like to shout it from the rooftops. You should be proud of her, Lanie. I know I'll never forget her."

Lanie's eyes glowed like blue embers. "That's a pretty tribute, Ken, tantamount to a declaration. But your sudden high regard for my daughter does not vindicate your reprehensible behavior to me. Surely you don't imagine I'm just going to forget this, pretend it never happened? Luring my child into the wilderness, exposing her to all its dangers and horrors! And that Indian—"

"That Indian," Ken interrupted, "gave his life for your daughter, Lanie. That Indian threw himself between her and a rattlesnake, knowing he would catch the fangs. That Indian loved your daughter."

"You're insane! He was the guide—it was his duty to protect her. Beth didn't even know him."

"She knew him, Lanie. Believe me, she knew him."

The smoldering embers flamed. "Just what are you daring to imply, Kenneth Steele?"

"Oh, Lanie, for Christ's sake!" His hand smacked the library table in angry frustration. "You know exactly what I'm implying. Face it. For once in your narrow life, face something that's not exactly as you think it should be and expect it to be—yes, and believe you can *make* it be! Some things—not many, perhaps, but some—are simply beyond the power and control of money!"

The blow Lanie struck him was defensive reflex, returning wound and insult. "You bastard!"

His fleeting smile pitied her. "That doesn't change anything, my dear. Not a goddamn thing. Because there are also some things you can't change by will or desire, either. Those kids weren't strangers to each other, Lanie. If you hadn't insisted that your doctor sedate and confine Beth, she'd be telling you all this herself now. She didn't want to leave his body behind. I thought I'd have to knock her out to get her into that helicopter. And the minute she's able, she'll go to the reservation to visit Mark Carradine's grandfather. You'll have a hard time stopping her."

Weakened, drained colorless as if an artery had been severed in her body, Lanie sat down, murmuring, "Mark Carradine. The name does sound familiar."

"You don't remember, do you? You have a convenient memory for blocking out things you prefer to forget. I suppose it's possible to live a lifetime shutting out disagreeable thoughts from the mind and admitting only pleasing ones, rather like entertaining choice guests and ignoring others. I mentioned the name when we were discussing the barbecue to introduce me to the local hierarchy. I suggested that you invite Mark Carradine, as someone I felt we should both meet. He had another name, too. Little Wolf. I didn't know him then, but I knew about him."

"From Beth?"

Nodding. "She confided in me—either because you weren't available, or she was afraid."

For a moment he thought she would strike him again, but she only asked, as the reporters had, "What happened in the Thicket?"

"What do you mean, what happened? We were lost. We were hungry and thirsty. We scrounged for food and drank boiled baygall slop. We slept on the ground by a fire. We tried not to panic, to keep our heads and stay alive. We thought we might die in there, and one of us did."

"But that's not all, is it? That's not everything, the whole story. There's more, Ken, and you obviously don't care to tell me. So I must insist. Is there something between you and Beth?"

"No, not like you think, anyway."

Her gaze was implacable. "I don't believe you."

"Lanie, I'm half-dead. I've hardly slept four hours in forty-eight, and my mind is fuzzy. Don't grill me any more now, make me say things I don't mean. If I could just get some rest, borrow that sofa or even the floor for awhile—"

"There's a guest room upstairs," she relented. "Take a shower and scrape that grotesque brush off your face. Get some sleep. We'll continue this discussion in the morning."

"Don't you mean inquisition?"

"Oh, don't act crucified! I haven't said or done anything you didn't deserve. Did you expect me to fall on your neck in gratitude for my daughter's life, after you put it in jeopardy?" She took a cigarette from a teakwood box, replaced it without lighting it. "I'll call Furbusher and tell him to bring you some decent clothes. You look and smell like a tramp! A deputy brought your car into town—it's at the sheriff's office."

"Impounded?"

"Of course not." She turned away from him. "Go upstairs, Ken. There's a razor, and the maid will give you towels and whatever else you need. I'm tired myself, and the lawyers are waiting."

"For what, Lanie? To see if you have grounds for legal action against me?"

"I could have, you know. You took Beth without my permission, didn't you? And she's a minor, isn't she?"

"Good God, did you think I had kidnapped her?" She did not answer, and the enormity of her silence appalled him. "That's precisely what you thought, isn't it? And I suppose you were waiting to be contacted for ransom?"

"Don't be absurd! If I'd thought that I'd have called in the FBI, wouldn't I?"

"Not necessarily, if you feared bad publicity for yourself having to explain your involvement with me."

"Oh, you're insufferable!"

"Get something straight in your muddled mind, Lanie! I know I joked about kidnapping you in New Orleans—but if you seriously imagine I would ever consider it with either you or your child—well, you don't know me at all, Lanie, any better than I know you! I didn't kidnap Beth, nor did I 'lure' or persuade her to go anyplace with me. Ask her, why don't you? I don't think she'll lie to you."

"Nevertheless, you did take her in your car without my knowledge, Ken. I don't give a damn whose idea it was, you did wrong. But I'm not going to make a legal issue of it, Ken. I only want to protect Beth from any unpleasant repercussions. Just remember, the Indian's name is not to be associated with hers in any way whatsoever except guide."

Ken was astounded. A boy had given his life to protect her daughter's. The body in the shallow pit might be Beth's, and her greatest concern was adverse publicity. What kind of mother, what kind of woman, what kind of person was this?

The patient attorneys provided some insight.

They had already successfully defended her against the press and public, now they waited like servants for additional duty or dismissal. She could command such loyalty and subservience and probably demanded it. He bowed in chagrin and mock servility. "Your legal slaves await your orders, ma'am. If I may be excused, please?" he said and left.

In the nineteenth-century chamber upstairs, he completed the civilized rituals and ablutions, then surrendered himself to exhaustion and did not wake until the next morning, disturbed by a commotion across the hall.

CHAPTER TWENTY-TWO

Beth was up and dressed in jeans and poncho, struggling to get past her mother, who was blocking the exit and trying to reason with her. Mrs. Whitney, embarrassed by the clamor and confusion in her ordinarily peaceful household, telephoned for medical assistance, positive that both her daughter and granddaughter were in urgent need of treatment. She feared that Lanie had suffered a relapse in her neurosis, and that now Beth would also have a trauma to heal.

"Problems?" Ken asked, opening his door.

"Help me with this child," Lanie flung over her shoulder. "She's hysterical."

Ken moved into the room. "What is it, Beth? Can you tell me?"

"I'm not hysterical, Ken, and I'm not sick. I just want to go to the reservation."

"Do you think that's wise today, honey? The Indians won't expect it of you. Let his people have some private grief."

"Ken's right," Lanie said, grasping at straws. "Indians prefer to mourn their dead alone."

Beth's expression combined contempt and hostility. "How would you know that, Mother? How would you know anything about Indians or any other race except your own?" She turned pleading eyes and voice to Ken. "Please, can't you make her understand, why I must go to Mark's grandfather?"

"She's your mother, Beth."

"Didn't you tell her how it was with Mark and me?"

"I told her Mark loved you."

"That's only half of it. Do you hear, Mother? Only half! I loved Mark, too."

Lanie gestured irritably, dismissing such juvenile nonsense. "Don't be silly, Beth. Love? You're a child, and he was a boy."

"He was a man," Ken corrected. "He proved that to my satisfaction."

"Your satisfaction? What value do you think I'd place on your judgment now?"

"Nevertheless, Beth and I should pay our respects to Mark's grandfather. And if you'll let her go to the reservation, I'll take her."

"Over my dead body!" Lanie cried. "Do you honestly imagine I'd let her go anywhere with you ever again? I think you must both have lost your minds in the Thicket! Beth is more ill than she realizes and will need time to recuperate—"

Beth glared her resentment and defiance. "Thanks for trying," she told Ken. "You're a fool, Mom. And the worst part is, you'll probably never know just how big a fool you actually are. Now I wish you'd just go away and let me alone."

"Give me your word you won't try to leave?"

"You mean escape? I'd have to jump out a window, and this is the second floor. If I didn't break a leg, you'd have a posse after me in minutes. And then likely confined in a strait jacket in a nice padded cell in an exclusive sanitarium that doesn't integrate its patients."

Dr. Ramsey came on the double and administered another soothing injection, while Beth protested that she was being turned into a drug addict. She told Ken, "They'd have a fit if I wanted to smoke some pot, yet they stick needles of junk into me and think nothing of it. And I don't even have any pain to kill—not that kind, anyway. I guess Mom's back on her tranquilizers; she has a medicine chest full of sedatives, pep pills, barb for sleep, all prescribed for her health. I wonder what they're whispering about in the hall?"

"Medical consultation." Ken said.

"Trying to decide whether or not to put me away somewhere maybe? Back in the hospital?"

"I wouldn't think so," Ken said. "You're the healthiest one of the bunch."

When the doctor had gone, showing himself out, Lanie stepped into the room. "Feeling better, darling? Grandma's going to sit with you."

"Mother, I don't need a baby sitter."

No comment from Mother. "Ken, may I see you in the library, please?"

"Again?" he asked ruefully, but shrugged and deferred to her as had the medical and legal sycophants.

Lanie immured them behind the sliding doors. "Your car's out front, Ken. The deputy drove it over awhile ago, and Furbusher brought you some clothes. Why don't you go to the estate and relax a few days? The caretaker will guard your privacy. There's no hurry to settle our differences. But I'm sure we both have some serious thinking to do and can talk better when things are more normal."

"Things will never be more normal, Lanie. Too

much has happened not to affect our lives and relationship permanently. That tragedy in the Thicket was largely my fault—you're right about that. I shouldn't have taken Beth with me, no matter her wishes or intentions, and certainly not without your consent. But she wanted Mark and me to get acquainted, and I thought he was an experienced guide. Also I was at a low ebb emotionally, in a quandary, and wanted to get away somewhere and forget myself for a few hours, which was as long as I expected to be gone. Anyway, it's done and no amount of remorse or recrimination can undo it, and I'm not pleading for sympathy or understanding. However, I would like to rest a day or so before going back to New Orleans, if that's agreeable. I'm beat, and I still have some personal problems to solve and emotions to organize. You see, I'm not quite sure myself what happened in the Thicket. I only know I'm not the same person who went in there."

"Oh, good Lord, Ken! You didn't undergo some great metamorphosis in the bush—it's just a psychological hangover common after a close brush with death. I know, I've experienced it myself. I've been half-crazy with fear and worry, thinking Beth was dead. Had I known about Mark Carradine then, I might have gone completely mad. The thought of her being infatuated with an Indian, sneaking around to see him—well, obviously such a thought never occurred to me!"

"Obviously," Ken agreed. "But not because you're prejudiced or anything like that. A Coushatta just wasn't in your plans for your daughter." He paused and resumed wryly, "Wow, I can just imagine her debut and the accounts in the social columns. Miss Elizabeth Hall, daughter of Mrs. Brian Tyson Hall and the late great industrialist, granddaughter of Mrs. Arthur Whitney and the late great doctor, was escorted by her fiancé, Little Wolf, son of the late Big Wolf and squaw, grandson of Wise Wolf, of the Alabama-Coushatta Reservation in the Big Thicket of Texas . . ."

"You're mocking me," Lanie accused, picking up a book and laying it down again. The draperies were open now, the blinds admitting sunlight, and no reporters camped on the property; they were down at the Sheriff's Department waiting for the Law to return with on-the-scene details. "I'll admit I haven't given it much thought, Ken. I was born to a certain life-style and viewpoint with which I'm content and comfortable, so I've had no inclination or incentive to alter my perspective. Furthermore, I've had enough personal crises and upheavals to assume impersonal and universal ones. I only hope Beth won't be permanently affected by that tragic experience, turned into a racial fanatic because she considers Mark Carradine a martyr who must be venerated, if nowhere else, at least in her mind. I should hate to see her whole life changed, perhaps ruined, and even destroyed by that one unfortunate incident."

"And without actually voicing it, you're relieved that Carradine didn't survive?"

"That's a horrible thing to say!"

"But true, Lanie, and truth is sometimes horrible. You couldn't have coped with a situation like that. You'd have disposed of that Indian somehow, as effectively as that snake did. You'd have kept him at bay, even if you had to declare war on his whole tribe. And you'd react the same way if ever Beth showed an interest in anyone but another WASP. Like mother, like daughter. You were born in your mother's image, Lanie, and you expected Beth to be born in yours."

Lanie flexed her hands, tense and nervous, striving to suppress her aggravation. "I realize you haven't fully recovered from your ordeal, Ken, and I'm trying to make allowances. But my patience has limits, and you're deliberately provoking me."

"Oh, hell, Lanie! You're fencing on the real issues, and you know it. At nineteen and sixteen, those kids had something neither of us has ever had, singly or together. They were in love, sure, but that's not all. They *liked* each other too, and maybe that's even more important than loving. They related, their feelings—vibrations—were in harmony, they *cared*, not only about themselves but others, and that's important, too. Mark's real heroism was in putting someone else before himself. He'd probably have done the same for me or anyone else threatened by danger, and that makes him special. And the way Beth nursed him, kept a vigil, worried and wept over him, helped to dig his grave with her bare hands—well, she considered Mark before herself, which makes her special also. And you don't want to connect them at all, not even associate her name with his!"

"I explained—"

"Be quiet," Ken said brusquely. "I'm not finished. All you were interested in is what you wanted for your daughter, not what she wanted for herself. And no doubt what you wanted out of marriage was more important than what your husband wanted, too. Most of the misery and unhappiness in this world has been caused by selfish, self-centered people and governments that put themselves before others. It's a human failing, unfortunately, natural enough, and I've been as guilty of it as anyone else. Beth made a rather profound observation in the Thicket, when she said there was a bigger one out here than in there. Pretty perceptive for someone her age."

"Out of the mouths of babes?" Smiling lamely, "My daughter made quite an impression on you, didn't she?"

"Indelible."

"And she was quite an education?"

"Priceless," Ken acknowledged. "I went into the Thicket feeling sorry for myself, because I thought life had betrayed me, and hence I didn't owe anyone anything any more, not even myself. And maybe the coward in me wanted to escape and be left in the wilderness, because I wasn't sure I could cope with it in civilization. You see, for thirty-six years I had been measuring my worth to society by my color and accomplishments. Then suddenly I was faced with an entirely different set of values and had to reorganize my thinking, refocus my perspective. For your sake, I even tried to convince Beth that the Indian was wrong for her, and she should forget him. Then the accident happened. And watching her with him, her tender care and devotion centered in the pure and simple love of one human being for another—well, it was a beautiful sight, Lanie. So inspiring I found myself envying a dying Indian."

"That's mawkish," Lanie deprecated. "The Thicket is noted for its legends and myths, and I suppose you and Beth and Mark Carradine have created another one. But it's over now, Ken. Time to come out of the jungle."

"I did," he said quietly.

"What?"

"I have a letter, Lanie. It'll explain everything."

She completely misunderstood. "Is it by any chance a confession? About . . . about Michele?"

Shaking his head sadly, "You were never convinced about that, were you? In addition to everything else there'd always be that doubt and suspicion between us. Maybe all this happened for the best, Lanie. We couldn't have made it together, not in a hundred years. I realize that now. It would have been foolish, stupid to try."

"You're raving, Ken. Not making sense. Some breakfast might help. I'll call Maple."

"Don't bother—I think I can find the servants' quarters. That instinct should be inherent in my blood."

"What instinct?"

"Servitude. Maple and I may even be related, in fact." And abruptly, because it seemed the best way and he was weary of dissembling, he said, "My great-grandparents were slaves. Yes, my dear, you heard me right. Slaves."

Her expression was unforgettable. Horror, at first; then revulsion and self-disgust. The dilemma that appalled every genteel white lady at the thought of surrendering to or being raped by a black man. She'd lain with a Negro, and there was no worse shame or scandal or debasement. She'd been defiled, contaminated, and how was she ever to purify herself again? Retraction was impossible, so perhaps denial and rejection . . .

"That can't be!"

"It can be and it is, Lanie. I'm a quadroon. The letter will tell you."

She sat down, or rather collapsed in a leather chair, clutching the arms tightly and murmuring, "Letter, letter—what letter?"

Ken explained and knew she was still loathe to

believe and accept and assimilate. "Beth knows, Lanie. I told her. She said it didn't matter to her. It's nothing disgraceful, you know. It's not a crime to be black."

"My God," she whispered, self-absorbed. "Oh, my God! Beth and an Indian, and me and a—a . . ."

"Nigger," Ken finished brutally. "You can't even say the terrible word, can you? It sticks in your throat and chokes you. It's like blasphemy to you and your mother, isn't it? And it would probably be easier to accept me as a murderer or kidnapper or embezzler or degenerate—anything but a Negro! You didn't know it when we were making love and neither did I if that's any consolation, so you didn't mind, you even enjoyed it. And you might still tolerate me as a lover, because my skin isn't black nor the rest of my anatomy. Funny, you don't look nigger, right? But the thought of me as a husband and possible father of octoroon children is abhorrent, isn't it? You'd never consider that!"

Lanie did not answer. He wasn't sure she'd even heard him. She was staring at the Persian carpet as if she'd never seen it before, or its intricate pattern fascinated and hypnotized her. A figure suddenly petrified and immobile as a marble statue.

"Lanie?" He touched her shoulder gently. No response. "Are you all right?"

When finally she spoke, her wistful voice and plea, like a naughty child afraid of maternal punishment, astonished him. "Don't tell Mother, please."

Is that all she could say? Was that her only concern, keeping it from her mother? My God, she was a pathetic child! The daughter was ten times, a hundred times, more a woman.

"Lanie?" He tried again to reach her, waiting in silence for silence. She had drifted into some kind

of trance or emotional catalepsy. There was no hope
of penetrating it, no point even in trying. He said,
"I'll get my things from the estate and be on my
way." Still catatonic. "Goodbye, Lanie. I'm sorry
for everything. Everything, believe me."

And again she begged, like an automaton pro-
grammed for repetition, "Please don't tell Mother."

CHAPTER TWENTY-THREE

His bags were packed and he was drinking a toast to the road when Beth arrived, her mount saddled and cantering slowly up the pine-spired avenue. Remembering the first time he had watched her lively approach, her dispirited posture now wrenched Ken. She had no business being out of bed, much less riding a horse. And how had she managed to escape her keepers, or had some other emergency developed to remove their guard? He met her at the door and drew her inside with both hands, eager and anxious.

"What're you doing here, Beth? I thought that hypo had knocked you out for the day?"

"No, it wore off a couple of hours ago. I didn't want to stay there." She indicated the luggage. "You were leaving without saying goodbye?"

"It seemed expedient," Ken said. "Does your mother know you left the house?"

"I think so, but I don't really care—and neither does she, now. Mom's in some kind of state. Dr. Ramsey is with her and consulting the Houston shrink long distance, and Grandma's blaming you for everything. She says it was a dark day when you entered our lives."

250

"Black," Ken said ruefully.

"You told Mom?"

"I told her."

"And she threw you out, just like I predicted?"

"I threw myself out. She couldn't. She was in shock."

"She might have another breakdown," Beth frowned. "Don't you care about that, Ken?"

"Oh, Beth, of course I care! But what do you think would have happened if I'd married her in spite of everything, with my 'dark secret' intact? You know how she reacted to you and Mark together, how bitterly she would have opposed your marriage. I could have lied to her successfully for awhile maybe, masqueraded my true identity like other colored passers. But eventually I'd be exposed, unmasked somehow, and she'd probably flip completely and hopelessly. Especially if by then the situation seemed irrevocable and irreparable in her mind, if she were pregnant or already had my child. She'd hate my guts! I couldn't risk that, Beth. Besides, there are other impediments now."

"Like what?"

His eyes brooded over her. "Impediments."

"But I don't want you to go, Ken!" She climbed onto the barstool beside him, as if sheer proximity could restrain him. She wanted a sip of his drink, and he held it to her mouth. "I won't have anybody I can talk to, who might understand or care about what I want to do."

"What do you want to do?"

"Start a memorial fund for Mark."

"Will his body be returned to the reservation?"

Another fortifying swallow of whiskey. "I don't know. Doc Ramsey said he heard that the sheriff will leave the decision to Mark's grandfather and the tribe. And since the Big Thicket will likely be a National Park someday, they might elect to leave Mark there and just put up a commemorative plaque or something." Talking about it hurt, deeply, and she tried to alleviate the pain with more bourbon. "He should have a monument, don't you think?"

"Yes, I do, Beth."

"I know the school kids will contribute, and lots of townspeople, too. Mom and Grandma would have to donate generously, to show their appreciation for what he did for me. They have historic markers all over this county—to trail blazers and scouts and cattle drivers, pioneers and frontier heroes, even to some famous outlaws, and Grandma was the ramrod of most of them. I'd like a bronze statue of Mark ten feet tall on the square, but I'm sure the Indians would prefer something simple. Doesn't matter, I guess, long as he's remembered. But people have to be reminded with material things, otherwise they forget. And I don't want Mark Carradine forgotten, ever."

"He won't be, Beth, with you in charge. I know your determination, perseverance, dedication. I've seen you in action, remember? You don't give up easily."

"I wish I could say the same for you."

"Now, Beth, we've been through all that."

"Don't worry, I'm not going to rap on it any more. Besides, I think now you did the right thing, after all. The decent, honest thing."

"Right or wrong, the only thing," Ken said.

"Sure, and I had to tell you. That's why I came. And I'm glad I did, if only to say goodbye. Can I write to you?"

"I'd be pleased."

"Will you answer?"

"Yes, but you may not always receive my answers."

"You mean my censors might intercept them?"

He said, "I may not even mail them."

"Oh," she murmured. "Oh, I think I understand." She paused, as though to organize her faculties for a strategic maneuver. "I plan to go to college in New Orleans. Tulane, if I can qualify."

"When did you decide that? You didn't mention Tulane in the Thicket."

"Well, I've decided now. And if I do go to Tulane, maybe we'll see each other sometime?"

"Maybe," Ken nodded.

"I hope so," she said. "What will you do when you get back?"

"What I did before, probably. I don't know. I'm pretty strung out right now." He lit a cigarette with shaking hands.

"I guess I am, too. Strung out, I mean. I think a part of me died with Mark and was left in the Thicket with him and will always remain there, and I'll have to find a replacement somewhere, somehow. Maybe my heart will divide and grow whole again, like an ameba. Only amebas don't have souls, so I'll have to revive my spirit myself."

"You don't lack heart or soul, Beth. You never did. And you have more than enough spirit, too. That experience in the Thicket didn't deplete your virtues, honey; if anything, it increased them."

"I just don't know why it had to happen, Ken. Why Mark had to die so young, and you have to go away now when I need you so much. Life is so rotten at times."

Ken touched her shoulder in a comradely way. "It gets worse with age."

"Oh, you're not so old."

"Twenty years your senior, my dear."

"Well, that's not even a generation, if a generation is twenty-five years. And I don't feel like a kid any more. I grew up in the Thicket."

"What a lesson in maturity," Ken reflected grimly.

"Yeah, some tough seminar."

Beth was surveying the magnificent room, as if to orient herself in unfamiliar environs; she had forgotten much of the opulence. "Do you like this place, Ken?"

"You want the truth? It scares hell out of me."

"Me, too," Beth admitted. "It didn't when I was little, because it was my home and I took it for granted. Kids do, you know, whether they live in splendor or squalor. But when I grew older and realized the difference in my home and other people's, I got sad and sick. Why so much for me, I wondered, and so little for others? Why did we give baskets to the poor at Christmas and forget them the rest of the year? Why was Grandma so absorbed in the past when the present was so much more important? What had we done to deserve such rewards and blessings? Nothing. It was all inherited—and my parents accepted it as their birthright. We were entitled through succession, like kings to a throne. Parasites in paradise! I never want to live here again."

"I can understand that, Beth. It's overwhelming, isn't it? I was even awed by my last wife's town house. But this palace! Maybe it's because some of my ancestors lived in grass huts, shanties, and slave cabins."

"So what? All our ancestors lived in caves, didn't they? Or maybe trees, if you swing with Darwin. Mark's were wigwam and hogan dwellers." She fondled the medallion around her neck, the imitation sabia which she had removed as a memento before the Indian's burial. "Mother forbade me to wear this, called it superstitious and barbaric. But I'll keep it always. And I wish I had something to remember you by, too. Give me a token, Ken."

He smiled, smoothing her hair from crown to waist. "Take my heart, little girl. Cut your wisdom teeth on it and keep me informed of your progress, even if you don't hear from me."

"I'll hear," she said confidently. "And sometimes I'll talk to you on the phone, even if I have to call collect. Good therapy for both of us. Besides, you'll want to know how the memorial fund is coming, won't you?"

"Sure, and I'll contribute—you know that."

Beth borrowed his drink, since he wasn't consuming it himself. "Two days ago I expected to die in the Thicket and didn't much care. But I feel a little better and different now. Maybe life, rotten and vile as it is sometimes, isn't all bad. And maybe there was some divine pattern or purpose for what happened. I have to believe that, since nothing else makes much sense. Does it?"

"Not much, no."

"When're you leaving, Ken?"

"Right after you do," he said. "And I think the time for that is now, Beth. Come, I'll see you off."

She hesitated, as if she had more to say, more than she could ever say, but she went obediently. "Will you kiss me goodbye?"

"No, darling, I won't."

"Should I ask why not?"

"No, darling, you shouldn't."

Outside, pacing her steps to his, deliberately delaying the inevitable, she said with her acute and often startling perception. "This house isn't the only thing that scares you, is it?"

Ken didn't answer. They had reached Brute. He boosted her up into the western saddle. "No bareback today?"

"I wasn't sure I could hang on," she said. "And I didn't want another bad fall on top of everything else. Like when I was twelve—remember I told you?—and tried to hide my bruises from Mom. But she saw them then, and I think she sees them now too, even if she won't admit it."

"Poor bruised baby," Ken said. "Try not to break your precious neck before you get your wisdom teeth," and slapped the horse into action before the rider could reply.

At the end of the road, Beth turned and waved at him, more a salute than a farewell, and then disappeared into the trees. It was getting late, almost sundown. Long shadows, but above the forest, still a lingering light. He could travel a fair distance before dark.